I0659196

Indiscriminate: 5th Anniversary Revised Edition

Riverdale PD Series

J.I. O'Neal

Published by RiverWalk Press, 2017.

This is a work of fiction. Similarities to real people, places, or events are entirely coincidental.

INDISCRIMINATE: 5TH ANNIVERSARY REVISED EDITION

First edition. December 9, 2017.

ISBN: 978-1393134428

Written by J.I. O'Neal.

This book is dedicated to:

My family,

The Thistles,

And all rescue personnel. You are all heroes.

CHAPTER ONE

———

"2259, BE ADVISED THIS is a possible 187. Suspect is possible 417, armed suspect. Proceed with utmost caution. Over."

Joyce. He could always tell when it was Joyce on the other end of the radio. She was the only dispatcher who didn't sound entirely like a machine, who used words like 'utmost' in her transmissions. Detective Sergeant Noah Harkham, badge number 2259, gripped his radio and punched down the button, gritting a reply to Joyce's warm, human voice. "I copy, Dispatch. No 101's on this one, my dear, word of honor. Over."

"I'll hold you to that, 2259." He could hear her smiling. "Standing by."

The radio went silent. Harkham slipped the handset onto his belt and inserted the tiny speaker, referred to as an earwig, into his right ear. He drew his gun, keeping his finger outside the trigger guard at the ready. He glanced to his left, past the overflowing garbage can that contained, if the smell was any indication, at least ten pounds of rotten fruit, to the uniformed officer crouched in the alley next to him – Officer Kenneth Stiles. He was an older cop who Harkham knew had good instincts, someone he could trust to keep it together if things went south – and he looked as miserable and hot as Harkham felt, adjusting his body armor to keep it from plastering to his sun-pinked skin.

Stiles held his Smith and Wesson Model 19 likewise at the ready. Why on earth Stiles had decided to keep the old thing after the department had gotten the money to equip its uniformed officers with the newer, sleeker semi-automatic M&P model, was the subject of much water cooler debate amongst most cops. Maybe he liked the dramatic sound of the hammer cocking, a feature the hammerless M&P lacked. When this thing was over, he'd be sure to ask.

No 101s, Harkham chanted mentally, wiping sweat from his brow. That wasn't standard code, not something in the manuals. It was a personal code that Joyce had coined. Translation: don't go acting like some cocky rookie who just walked out of your first class at the Academy thinking you know it all – when you don't – that you end up screwing everything up. And it was what she told him when he got called to his first scene over twelve years ago.

Joyce, a detective's widow, had been with the precinct for more years than she'd care to admit to and was a sort of 'mother hen' to Harkham and his colleagues. He wouldn't tell just anyone, but hearing her voice in his ear did more to calm his hammering heart and steel his nerves as he prepared to enter a bad situation than all of his training and mental preparation combined.

The crowd that would have been strolling up and down the sidewalks of this area was being held at bay until this was over. People were standing under the awnings of the surrounding businesses to escape the afternoon sun, too curious about what was going to happen to seek air conditioning.

He caught Officer Stiles' eye and raised one dark eyebrow. Stiles nodded, his pleasant face turned serious with dark brows pulled low, shading his eyes the color of coffee. Harkham nodded in reply and signaled the other group, comprised of Officers Adelmo and Cox, and headed by Harkham's partner, Detective Alan Franks - AKA, Frankie, who all huddled behind a patrol car across the street from the apartment building's main entrance.

Frankie's' dirty-blond hair was darkened by sweat, his eyes blue slivers as he squinted against a glare. Cox's fair skin and hair made him almost glow in the bright sunlight, especially contrasted with Adelmo's dark, Italian complexion.

Harkham held up three fingers. He curled down one...then a second...then he dropped the last finger and shouted, "Go!"

Harkham and Stiles charged up the fire escape to the fourth floor apartment where Bobby Avalon, a semi-famous heavyweight boxer, was reportedly holed up after firing a gun and shouting threats to everyone within earshot.

What none of them knew was whether or not the boxer's girlfriend was still on the premises. She had called the precinct fifteen minutes ago saying her drunk and high boyfriend, Bobby Avalon - you know, *the* Bobby Avalon - had assaulted her after coming back from a drug score. She had been advised to leave the apartment if possible and go to a neighbor's place to wait for the ambulance to arrive, but had not stayed on the line until it could be verified she had complied.

However, several people had reported hearing shouting followed by a single gunshot, and then more yelling, just moments before Harkham and his team showed up. They were treating this as a domestic violence situation that had possibly turned deadly.

Harkham and Stiles dropped low and hugged the wall by the fire escape window, the rough brick snagging at their Kevlar vests, pausing long enough to allow Frankie and the officers to get to the door and identify themselves. Peering through the window, he saw the suspect, sitting on the once-stylish living room couch, stagger to his feet.

"Get outta here!" Avalon shouted. His paunch bulged under his tee shirt, but the boxer's arms and shoulders were still muscular enough to leave no doubt as to how he'd earned the nickname 'The Mallet.'

"Riverdale Police!" Frankie repeated. "Open the door or we're breaking it down!"

Avalon looked around, frantic, then bent down to retrieve the gun from the floor next to the couch. "Suspect is armed!" Harkham cautioned into the radio. "I repeat, 417 confirmed." He tried to line up a shot at Avalon, but the boxer moved just enough to inadvertently place his kitchen wall between himself and the detective. "I can't get a clean shot," he advised Frankie. "Move in."

Then, Frankie's and Harkham's teams entered the apartment simultaneously – Frankie's by breaking down the door and Harkham's by breaking the window. The inebriated suspect was confused by the two-pronged attack, allowing the cops to take advantage of that time and surround him. Guns were leveled at him and orders to drop his weapon were shouted at the boxer from all sides. Avalon hesitated, then swung the gun up and pointed it at Officer Adelmo's chest.

Harkham – unable to take a shot without endangering Cox opposite him – shouted a warning and lunged at Avalon, knocking him to the ground.

The gun went off.

The bullet lodged into the wall near the top of the window. But it was Officer Cox who collared Avalon, because everyone else was too preoccupied by a screaming, bleeding Noah Harkham, who lay on the floor clutching the left side of his face in agony.

––––––––––––

"2259, 2914, REPORT!" JOYCE demanded. "Advise your status."

"Officer down! Officer down! 10-52 - get a rescue unit up here now!" Frankie threw down his radio and was at his partner's side in an instant. "Harkham! Hark, are you hit? Are you hit? Let me see, let me see," he wrestled Harkham's hands away from his face.

Burnt gunpowder stippled his temple, imbedded into his skin in a jagged, elliptical pattern. The flesh around his left eye and back to his ear had been seared by the gun's propellant gases, melting it like candle wax. His grey eyes were shut and tears ran red and black to disappear into his black hair. Blood oozed from his ear canal. Harkham's even features were now contorted in agony, and he groaned and shook with pain.

Frankie cursed, his voice shaking.

"God Almighty, no," Adelmo breathed, making the sign of the cross.

Stiles made a sweep of the litter-strewn apartment and came back into the living room, unable to stop staring as Frankie held Harkham's hands to keep him from clawing at his wounds.

"No sign of the girl," he reported.

Cox held the suspect subdued beneath his body weight and the boxer was laughing and screaming in mockery of Harkham. "SHUT UP!" Cox ordered, jerking Avalon by the back of his collar and slamming his face into the dirty beige carpet.

"Frankie," Harkham groaned, grasping the other detective's shirt in a vise grip. "I can't...I can't...what just happened?"

Cox and Stiles dragged the boxer – who was unscathed except for being higher than the pigeons roosting on the rooftop - to his feet and out of the apartment to the patrol car downstairs. Adelmo stepped into the hall to direct the paramedics in.

They administered a sedative and assessed Harkham's wounds before loading him up on the gurney. He was unconscious now, more from pain and shock than medication, and the medics carried him down to the waiting ambulance. Frankie followed close behind.

"You're gonna be all right, Hark," Frankie muttered over and over on the way down the long flights of stairs and all the way to hospital.

———————————

"YOU'RE GOING TO BE all right, Detective Harkham," a voice reassured him.

Lights overhead flashed by in rapid succession. Faces swam in and out of sight. Voices faded in and out. He tried to listen to them, but he couldn't concentrate. He knew he was lying on something that felt like a bed, but he seemed to be moving. There were people all around him, focusing on him, but he couldn't quite focus on them. The more he tried to think through the fog in his mind, the more he felt lost in it.

"– cochlear damage –"

Behind it all was a ringing he couldn't account for.

"– the cornea is ruptured -"

Something wet and heavy lay across half his face, but he didn't seem able to reach it.

"– retina is detached –"

It felt like he was in a dream.

"– severe searing, the burns are pretty bad – "

He realized his arms felt heavy, or hindered, and resisted his efforts to move them, but he didn't know why. He might have been able to figure it out if he could concentrate, but the ringing was too distracting. It sounded like the test pattern alert when a television station went off the air at four a.m.

"– likely be severely scarred –"

He tried to tell them to turn off the TV, to turn it off so he could hear. So he could think, to remember, because it was important. Something had gone wrong, something...

"Adelmo," he said, his voice croaking. The gun, he remembered: it was aimed at Adelmo. It was too close, too close and if it had gone off the vest might not have caught the bullet, might not have saved him. "Adelmo?"

"One of the officers," someone said.

"Everyone else is just fine, Detective," another voice told him. "Everything will be all right; we're going to take care of you."

No, he wanted to say, not me. Help Adelmo. But Adelmo was fine, they said.

With a strangely loud yet muffled thump, he passed through a set of double doors and the sharp smell of gunpowder – which had been filling his nose for what seemed like forever now – was joined by a different, harsher smell. Chlorine? Ammonia? He wasn't sure what it was, but it filled him with unnamed terror and he wanted very much to be somewhere else, anywhere else, because he knew they were wrong. Everything would not be fine because something had gone terribly wrong.

Something terrible had happened to *him*.

CHAPTER TWO

———

"OKAY, MR. HARKHAM," the ophthalmologist said with his usual cheeriness, "I want you to keep your eyes on the knot of my tie and tell me when you can no longer see my finger. Okay?" Doctor Joseph Barnes regarded Noah with his friendly cornflower-colored eyes, his flop of nut-brown hair almost brushing his eyelashes.

Noah managed a weak smile and a nod. The doctor held up one slim finger far to the right of Noah's head. "You can see it over here, can't you?"

"Yes."

"Good." The doctor slowly moved his finger in front of Noah's face, to the middle, then to the left.

"Stop," Noah said. "There. I lost it there."

The ophthalmologist's finger froze just past Noah's left eye, where the peripheral vision of his right eye ended. He frowned, making his face look prematurely aged. "Let's try one more test, shall we?" He kept his tone cheerful, but his body language was stiff, his smile forced.

"No need," Noah replied. "We both know the results."

"None of that, Noah," Doctor Barnes chided. "We'll try another." He handed Noah a black plastic spoon-like instrument. "Cover your right eye."

Noah sighed and put the spoon over his good eye. He was plunged into darkness and felt his pulse and breathing quicken. A click told him Doc had killed the lights.

"Deep breaths, Noah," Barnes murmured. "I'm going to take a look at the back of your eye now."

Noah took a deep breath and held it a moment while Doctor Barnes examined his ruined eye. He could feel the man's proximity, could smell his minty breath, but he could not see him.

"Your eyes are darting," Barnes complained. "I need you to try to keep them still."

"Sorry," Noah replied, struggling to keep his eyes from moving.

"What did the audiologist say yesterday?" Dr. Barnes asked.

Noah's fingers clenched tighter around the plastic handle. "It's permanent. The damage is beyond repair. I'll never hear out of that ear again."

Barnes paused. "I'm sorry."

"Yeah," was all Noah could say.

Barnes commenced the exam. After a long moment he stopped again. "Okay. Keep your right eye covered. I want to test for involuntary reactions."

Noah jerked the spoon away from his eye. "Like what?"

"Hmm? 'Like what' what?"

"Tell me what you're going to do. In case you haven't realized, with this thing over my good eye, I'm completely blind." Vulnerable, phobic. "I want to know what to expect."

"I'm going to flick lights of varying intensities across your eye to check if you are able to pick any up."

Noah felt a surge of hope. "Does that mean the retina is looking better?"

"Well," he said with a sigh, the light from the ophthalmoscope throwing a yellow-white arc across his furrowed brow, "we know the last surgery to reattach the retina was mostly successful, but there is a lot of scar tissue yet. But the new cornea is looking very good, so I'm thinking the eye is trying to repair itself. I just need a way to measure any progress."

Noah's heart lurched. "You're saying there is a chance I could see again?"

"It's been nine months, Noah, and three surgeries with no significant recovery of vision. The scar tissue is still prolific and we know now that the damage was more extensive than we had initially thought, but there are signs of healing. Perhaps someday down the line you will regain some visual ability."

"That sounds a lot less promising than it started out." He tried to keep the bitterness and disappointment out of his tone, and met with partial success.

"I told you when we first met I would never be less than honest with you. Brutally if I had to. Hope is a wonderful thing to have and can speed recovery. But it is a terrible thing when it is false and can do irreparable damage. I won't give out false hope and I won't let you harbor any."

Noah stared at the spoon in his hands, a slightly darker black against the blackness of the darkened room. "That's why I agreed to let you be my doctor." He lifted his head and fixed his gaze on the tidy knot of Barnes' cerulean tie. "Let's try that test, shall we?" He was once again plunged into phobic darkness as the spoon blotted out his sight.

CHAPTER THREE

———

"Though this be madness, yet there is method in't."

Shakespeare, Hamlet

HIS BREATHING WAS STARTING to rasp in his throat, which felt as sticky wet as his mouth felt bone dry. He steadied himself with one hand on the uneven concrete blocks and took three deep, slow breaths, working his tongue to moisten his mouth. Now. Now was the moment. He'd been waiting a long time for it and could hardly believe it had actually come at last.

The window was open. It would be simple, so simple. And quick, not like it had happened to them. He regretted that, the quickness. If he had his way it would be otherwise, but the situation necessitated swiftness.

He took a minute to drink in his surroundings, to savor everything about this moment. His hands were now steady. His pulse and breathing returned to normal. No panic crept up his spine; no doubts beat their wings against the walls of his mind. The street lay silent and grey below, three stories below. It didn't seem that far, but it was far enough to do the trick.

He stared through the window. With a deep breath, he closed his eyes and plunged forward.

His feet made contact with the floor. With a small snick he released the mechanism on the harness and felt the rope go slack. Paying out the necessary length, he crept across the boards, willing his movements to go unheard. Beds lined the two longest walls, the forms of their sleeping occupants rendered shapeless in the thick shadows. Anonymous.

It didn't matter who they were anyway - they each had some part in it. They all needed to be punished. An indiscriminate penalty for an indiscriminate crime. The two beds on either side of the window were empty, as were several others around the room. Two large ceiling fans churned overhead, two pedestal fans oscillated on opposite ends of the room, stirring the stuffy air. The sleeper in the corner snored.

He smiled bitterly at their oblivious forms. A fire alarm would be the only thing to wake these guys up. Nevertheless, he moved in silence across the floor to the wall opposite the window. First thing, he had to make sure his message would be received. Then, and only then, did he allow himself to indulge in the creating.

He piled the items into the middle of the floor. He would have preferred to spend more time with this, to bring it into the world properly, but he didn't have that luxury. His heart raced as the first spark of life bloomed into something more. The most primal of beings, the most beautiful of beasts.

How he longed to stay and watch it fulfill its purpose. But he had to leave. With a heavy heart, he reeled in the slack rope, then climbed out the window and ascended to the roof. Down the fire escape and into the darkness of the sleeping city streets. Home free.

He paused in the shadows to glance up once more at the historic brick building. A symbol of peace of mind. It was robbed of that peace now, and he was the thief.

That's when he heard the dog growl. There was a man with the animal, one who wasn't sleeping like he was supposed to be. The man called out, asking who was there. The dog began to bark.

No, it couldn't end this way. He darted from the shadows toward the street. Panic was starting to return. Stay focused. Get away.

The man and the dog were right behind him, faster than he was. He wasn't going to make it, so he stopped just at the sidewalk and turned. The gun was in his hand almost before he consciously thought of it. A warning shot, that's all he needed. Something to scare them off. He held his breath and squeezed the trigger.

The dog yelped and ran. The man went down, oddly quiet. He was no more than ten feet away, lying in the damp grass, eyes closed. A pool of scarlet was spreading across the middle of the man's torso, far more blood than he even imagined possible, and the panic started to creep back in. He had to remain calm, in control. No matter the outcome, it was the message that was important. They had to know. He had to make them see it.

From the yelling and alarms coming from inside, he knew he had already succeeded.

He turned and ran, letting the shadows erase him from sight.

CHAPTER FOUR

———

DETECTIVE FRANKS SWEPT his gaze around the scene. Nine firefighters stood huddled in the crowded street outside the station house. Officers were having a time of it trying to keep night-gowned and p.j.-clad neighbors and looky-loos behind the tape line. He sighted another news crew van rolling in and groaned inwardly.

Not for the first time he wished Hark were here. The crime scene unit had been called twenty minutes ago and still hadn't shown up yet. Used to they wouldn't've even called them. Harkham had graduated from Riverside University with a Bachelor's degree in Forensic Science and had always processed his own scenes, an arrangement granted by their superior, Captain Ziehring. Of course, everything he collected from a scene was then handed over to the crime lab, but it was so much more efficient when they didn't have to wait for the CSIs.

"Finally," he muttered, seeing the black mobile response vehicle pull up. Three people climbed out of the van, each clutching a black evidence kit. Frankie gave them a grim nod by way of greeting.

"Quite a turn out," commented the senior CSI, Cal Parker, his hazel eyes alight with excitement, though his expression maintained a proper scientific detachment. "Here's hoping they haven't trampled all over anything useful."

"The scene is secure; we've kept everyone out of the grass. But some of our guys have been up there," he nodded to the fire station.

"All right. Conrad, take the perimeter and make sure you get exclusionary shoeprints from everybody who's been on the scene."

Conrad Ward, a sun-bleached blond Californian who reminded
Frankie a little of a young Henry Fonda – but sounded more like
pro-skater Tony Hawk – nodded. "Right, I'm on it." He tapped
Frankie's slight paunch with his knuckles. "How 'bout we start with
you, Frankie?" Ward asked, his blue-green eyes smiling at the detective.

Frankie grumbled to himself. Ward was a good CSI, granted, but his
laid-back air irritated him. It felt like Ward had a lack of respect and
professional interest, even though Frankie knew that wasn't the case.
Ward was dedicated to his work, and took every scene, every crime very
seriously. His easy smile and levity was just his way of staving off the
burnout that seemed to have afflicted others in his line of work. But
still...

"Do we know how he got in?" Parker asked, furrowing his graying
brown eyebrows.

"The firefighter who called it in said there was an open window on
the third floor," Frankie answered. "Near as I can tell he came up the
fire escape and went in from the roof somehow. The guys who were
awake say no one triggered the alarm and didn't show up on the security
camera. They didn't hear the shot because of all the chaos upstairs. They
were too busy putting out the fire in the middle of the dormitory."

Frankie had been mentally going through his extensive movie
collection, trying to come up with a film that paralleled the unusual
crime that had taken place here tonight, and though there were some
that were similar, nothing was quite right. If Hollywood had made it,
he hadn't seen it. And that was saying something.

"Interesting," Parker commented. "I'll take the fire escape and roof, then, once I'm done with scene of the shooting. Neil, you take primary on the dormitory. Try to process whatever evidence wasn't destroyed by the fire." There seemed to be more to this simple request, an importance laid upon it Frankie missed.

"Got it," Neil Coates replied with similar profoundness. "Excuse me," he said as he slipped past Frankie and went into the station.

Neil was more of what a CSI should be, he thought: serious, insightful and analytical. He was a little too reserved, though; you could never tell what he was thinking. Everyone said he and his cousin, Noah Harkham, looked enough alike to be brothers. True, they did have the same dark hair and linear brow line, and similar mouths, but to Frankie the contrast in personality rendered the passing resemblance almost non-existent.

Parker was eyeing a trail in the grass next to the sidewalk. "Franks," he called, "tell me this isn't what I think it is."

Frankie stepped off the sheet of paper he had just imprinted with his size elevens. "What's that?"

"There are tire marks here. Thin, no tread. Tell me you didn't let them take the body before we got here."

Conrad gave him an incredulous look. "You gotta be kidding."

"Ambulance took him." The CSIs stared at him in disbelief.

"What?" Parker asked.

"The guy was still alive. They took him to the ER."

"How long ago?" Parker demanded, speed dialing his cell phone. "How long?"

"Maybe fifteen minutes ago. Why?"

Parker held up a finger as the call connected. "Robin, it's Cal. Listen: the shooting I have you on standby for isn't a DOA. The victim is at the ER now. I need you to get over there and make sure they extract the bullet without destroying it. All my CSIs are in the field – there's another case downtown – so I need you to do it yourself... Uh-huh. Thanks, Robin." He hung up.

"I'm sorry, Parker, they were supposed to have told you," Frankie said as the CSI headed for the fire escape. "Now on, I call you myself."

"See that you do, Franks."

CHAPTER FIVE

———

NEIL SLOWLY LOWERED the camera, still unable to believe what he was seeing. No one had said anything about the message scrawled across the wall in tight, angrily slanting letters written in what appeared to be permanent marker. *Too little...,* it read, but was it an accusation pointed at the victim, or those trying to save his life and find his attacker? Either way, it was obvious this guy had a grudge, and he wasn't shy about acting on it. He dialed Parker's cell phone.

"Whatcha got, Neil?"

"Cal, the attacker left a message."

"What? Where?"

"On the wall. I'm getting photos and a sample, but it looks like it's written in permanent marker. Says, 'Too little,' with an ellipsis after it, like there's more to the message. Nothing else is written here, though."

"Hmm...I don't like the sound of that. Okay, just make sure you get pristine photographs before sampling it."

"You got it, boss," he replied before hanging up. The scene was a mess, thanks to the firefighters' attempts to quell the fire that had been set in the middle of the floor. It was lucky the perpetrator had left the message, since it was likely to be the only intact evidence left to go on.

Neil removed his penlight from his kit and shone it around the scorched area. The two stripped beds told him the arsonist had improvised, using whatever was at hand to start the fire. If it was premeditated, it suggested he was used to improvising, which meant he may have done this before. And everything about this scene suggested it was premeditated.

He processed the rest of the area, ending with taking samples from the torched bed linens, before turning his attention to the window. This had to be the entry and exit point. If he had tried to come up from the ground floor, he would have tripped the alarm. And Frankie had said the preliminary review of the security cameras showed nobody coming or going during the night.

The window didn't give him much, either. There was a little bit of dirt on the ledge, like it had been scraped off of something, but nothing else he could see. He collected the dirt and dusted the whole frame for prints. Several smudges appeared, in the usual places you'd expect them if the window was routinely opened and closed. There was nothing useful here.

Heavy footfalls on the roof above preceded Parker calling out to him. "Hey, Neil?"

He stuck his head out the window and looked up at his boss. "Yeah?"

"Have you processed the window yet?"

"Just finishing up. Not much to go on. There wasn't much left of any use around the victim's bed or the ones he pulled the linens off of, either - the paramedics and firefighters pretty much obliterated any shoe prints or anything else he might've left behind. Does it still look to you like he came and went through here?"

"He had to have, don't you think?" Parker replied in his teaching voice.

He nodded. "No alarms tripped, nothing on the cameras, according to Frankie. No one saw or heard anything until the fire woke them up...it's the only thing that makes any sense."

Parker nodded. "You've just perfectly summed it up. And I found some navy blue fibers on the brickwork up here - material from a rope, maybe. There are two deep gouges in the brick near the top of the wall around the roof, each with a pile of powder below them."

"Like brick or mortar dust?"

"It's a safe assumption, but we'll have to test to confirm."

He thought this over, looking down to the ground and back up. "Grappling hook? Some kind of climbing gear?"

"That's what I'm thinking." Something seemed to catch his attention. "At the top of the window, just above you there, there's another bit of that navy colored fiber. See if you can get it without taking a dive, will you?"

"Sure thing." He ducked back inside and got a pair of long forceps and a small evidence bag. He then leaned back out, bracing himself on the window frame and reached up to snag the fibers. Carefully putting them into the evidence bag, he commented, "Good thing the wind is pretty dead tonight, or this might've blown away."

Parker nodded. "Let's hope the wind is the only thing dead tonight."

"Yeah... I'll get my stuff gathered up and meet you back downstairs, all right?"

"Take your time, I'm going to be up here another few, anyway."

He took the advice for its subtext rather than its surface meaning: *be extra thorough, don't give them any reason to criticize your work on this one, too.* The whole thing was making his blood boil, but, like he did with everything, he clamped down hard on it, keeping an outward placid expression.

As he was packing up his kit, however, he noticed his movements were jerky and he was closing and shoving things harder than necessary. And when he went to put his penlight into his pocket, he dropped it instead, its light flicking on and casting a long cone of yellow light sweeping across the floor.

He gritted his teeth and reached for it, but saw it was reflecting off of a dark object under one of the beds. As he got closer, he could see it was the cap of a marker, and likely the one used by the assailant. "Jackpot," he whispered, extracting the cap and getting it into an evidence bag.

His phone rang, startling in the quiet room. He stripped off his gloves and put them in his kit's biohazard container. "Hello?"

"Neil? It's Ashton."

He closed his eyes. "Yes, sir. What can I do for you?"

Ashton sighed. "They've decided to proceed. Monday morning, nine."

"But that's -" he took a breath and clamped down on the rest of that sentence. "Yes, sir."

"I did what I could, I want you to know that."

"I appreciate it, sir." He eyed the crime scene around him and nearly laughed at the irony of his situation. Nearly.

"Where are you right now?"

"The fire station scene."

"Stop. Whatever you've collected, give it to Parker. You don't necessarily have to go on leave at this point, but I can't have you on scene."

He gripped his phone hard enough to make his hand hurt. "Yes, sir." He hung up and just stood there, focusing on his breathing for several minutes, trying to quell his frustration. It wasn't working.

He grabbed his kit and left.

CHAPTER SIX

CONRAD KNELT IN THE grassy yard flanking the firehouse and took one more photograph of a promising looking shoe print. Then he mixed up a pack of dental stone to pour into the print and make a casting of it. This print, one of five he'd found leading from the fire escape south toward the street, was the clearest yet. The ground here was a little lower and was still damp from the fire station's sprinkler system - which he'd just learned had last gone off at 10 p.m. On first impression, these prints were from athletic-type shoes, roughly a size nine or ten.

The sound of footsteps made him look up from his work. Cal Parker came down the fire escape, searching it as he descended. Conrad stirred the dental stone mixture as he watched him a moment.

"Am I the only one who thinks it's ironic that there's a fire escape at the fire station?" Conrad asked with a grin.

Parker smiled, but never took his eyes off the textured metal steps. He stopped on the third from the bottom to peer closer at the surface. He pulled a gel lifter from his kit.

"Got a good one, boss?" Conrad asked, pouring dental stone into the shoe print.

Parker pressed the gel to the step surface and then glanced over at him. "Maybe. How about you?"

"One decent impression, four partials that aren't so good." He gestured to the set of evidence markers a few feet behind him. "Processed the victim's blood and found the shell casing. I had to fish it out of what I thought at first was just mud. Turns out it was old, soggy dog crap." He made a face, remembering the unpleasant aroma. "It'll have to be cleaned up before Shots can get anything useful out of it."

Parker frowned in sympathy. "That's lovely."

"Yeah. I got a lot of overlapping footprints around where his body was laying, all from the paramedics, I'm sure, though I'll have to get elimination prints from them, too, to be certain. But this one," he said, pointing to the casting, "is clear. Directionality alone shows it's our guy - all the prints lead from the fire escape, tending south to the street here."

He stood and surveyed the trail of the assailant's prints. "Looks like he gets to the sidewalk or the street and then turned to shoot the firefighter - all the prints in the yard go the same way. Then he just..." he gestured vaguely toward the opposite side of the street, "disappeared."

He eyed the area to the south. "There's a lot of city south of here. He could be anywhere by now." He turned back to his boss. "These impressions are less than stellar and look like they're from a fairly generic shoe. I don't see how we're gonna find this guy, Cal."

"Nay-sayer," Parker chided.

He shrugged. "That may be, but I'm still right and you know it. With no apparent motive, we better pray we get a fingerprint or DNA that's already in the system."

Parker looked up from the gel and fixed him with a look. "No apparent motive?"

"You don't need to give me The Eyebrow, boss - I'm just repeating what I was told. Frankie says the fire chief says all of his guys are stand up. Nobody had any problems with any of them, as far as he knew."

"Apparently, he was wrong," he replied and filled Conrad in on the message Neil had found on the wall.

"Too little..." he mused. "What's that supposed to mean?"

"I don't know. Yet." Parker looked around as if just then aware of their surroundings. "Where did everyone go?"

"Frankie had all the firefighters go down to the station to get their statement taken." He laughed, remembering the scene that followed. "You should've seen it - all the press people were pushing for a comment and trying to take pictures and all that, so Frankie tells 'em to clear off or he'd charge them with impeding his investigation. Of course that didn't deter 'em one bit, so he then says, 'I'll give an in-depth exclusive to the first crew that vacates the premises. You have twenty seconds.' Then he looks at his watch and says, 'Okay, go!' and they all took off like, like -" he searched for an appropriate simile.

"Race horses out of the gate?"

"Yeah," he laughed. "Then he told the looky-loos to go home and watch it on TV in the morning. All that's left is us and a few uniforms."

A half-smile drew up one side of Parker's mouth. "And here I never thought him that manipulative." He brought the lifted print over and showed it to Conrad. "It's just the front tip of the shoe, but the print is very clear. How's it compare?"

He examined it. "Yeah. Yeah, looks consistent. I'd say it's our guy." Movement at the front of the building caught his eye and he looked up to see Neil heading their way. "He looks happy," he said ironically.

To those who didn't know him as well, Neil didn't look any different. But Conrad saw the stiffness to his friend's shoulders and the slight furrow between his brows. Neil's steps were fast and heavy as he strode toward them with a small evidence bag clutched tightly in one fist and his kit in the other.

"We might have gotten lucky," he said, shoving the evidence bag at Parker.

"The cap to the marker used to write his message?"

"That's what I'm thinking. It'll have to be dusted for prints and swabbed for DNA." He opened his kit and took out all his other evidence bags, handing each of them to Parker. "Samples from the fire - he used the linens from a couple of empty beds. Not sure about any accelerants; doesn't look like he used any. There's the fiber bundle from the window. And there's the message he wrote," he added, handing over a section he'd cut out of the dry wall.

"Okay," Parker said. "That's all great work, but why are you giving it all to me?"

But before Neil could answer, Parker's phone rang. "Hold that thought," he said, walking away to answer it.

Conrad and Neil watched him a moment. "I hope that's Shots saying she got a clean bullet," Conrad said. Neil grunted noncommittally, so Conrad gave him a worried glance. "You all right? I mean, you're actually emoting."

Neil glared at the ground. "What are you talking about?"

"Hey, I just mean usually you're Mr. Placid, so even-keeled. But look at you, man: your jaw is clenched, your posture is stiff, and your tone is all angry. What's up?"

Neil sighed, then looked back up at Conrad. "Ashton just called me. They're going to go ahead with a formal internal affairs investigation," he said, his voice now flatter and more unemotional like normal. "He told me to hand everything over to Parker and leave the scene."

"What? But I thought everything was settled at the informal inquiry."

"So did I, but apparently someone wasn't satisfied. I put it down to the scumbag's lawyer." He shrugged and looked away.

"Listen: don't worry, all right? You didn't do anything wrong so you've got nothing to worry about."

"Yeah, but I've got nothing to prove Turner's story isn't true. If they have even the slightest doubt about me, I'm gone." His gaze strayed to Parker.

Conrad followed his gaze. "Cal's on your side. You know that, right? He's gonna do whatever he can to clear you."

"I'm not so sure even he'll be able to help me if they decide to fire me. But what gets me the most is, even if I am cleared, there's always going to be that nagging doubt, that 'what if?' in the back of everybody's mind. They can clear me, but they can't take away that taint."

"Everybody knows you're innocent. Everything's gonna go back to normal once this all blows over. You'll see. You just gotta relax. Don't let them stress you out over it."

"Yeah, well, easier said when it's not happening to you." He put a hand on Conrad's shoulder briefly, then took his kit back to the van.

CHAPTER SEVEN

NOAH DRUMMED HIS FINGERS on his thigh and glanced at the clock. He wanted to shout, what's taking so long? But he already knew the answer: Ziehring knew why he was here and was putting him off as long as possible. That was okay, he could wait. He had nothing but time these days.

Glancing through the reception room window into the hallway, he caught sight of a fondly familiar face. The lovely black woman stopped in mid-stride, smiling in the proud-mother way he remembered so well. He waved and she came through the door balancing a stack of paperwork, a purse and a large cup of coffee. He stood and helped her set all this aside, then embraced her.

"Oh, my boy," she said, giving him a squeeze. "Let me look at you." She held him at arm's length and scrutinized him head to toe.

"What's the verdict, Joyce?"

"Better, baby. Much better," she squeezed his arms. "You look good, Hark. How are you feeling?"

"Bored. Restless." He gave her a grim smile. "Pointless. Take your pick."

"I meant physically, but I know what you mean. I felt the same way after losing Danny. I missed this place, too. Missed the people, the community of it. That's why I took this job, to stay in touch and be part of the world that kept Danny so near its heart. Did I ever tell you that?"

"No, but somehow I knew that's what it was. And I'm glad. You're my anchor out there, Joyce. Or were. But I guess I broke my promise, didn't I?"

"What do you mean?"

"I promised you no 101s," he said quietly.

"Oh, honey," her eyes teared up, "don't you ever say that. You did not pull a 101 on me, Noah Harkham. You did a brave thing."

"I should have taken the shot, but I thought..." he shook his head. "Instead I knocked the guy to the ground and let him squeeze off a round. I put my whole team in danger."

She touched her fingertips to the scars on the left side of his face. "I think you're suffering enough without unnecessary guilt. Don't you?" She gave a small smile, then gathered up her things. "I'd best get back down in the trenches. Keep in touch, you hear me, baby?"

Noah nodded and she left the room. After she was lost to sight, he ran his own fingers across where he could still feel her touch. The scars from the gun's propellant gases felt hot and stretched tight, like pointing fingers, mocking his inadequacy. What was he doing here? What made him think things could ever be the way they were? He should leave, now, before the Captain called him into his office.

But then what? What would he do with his life if he walked away now?

He had to at least try to get his life back, right? But what would he do if Ziehring turned him away? He sighed, wrestling with what to do – leave and never know if he still had a chance or stay and face the possibility of his hopes being crushed?

But when Ziehring opened his door and called Noah's name, there really was no choice. He got up and entered the office.

"IT'S GOOD TO SEE YOU, Harkham," Ziehring said, shaking Noah's hand. "Have a seat."

Noah sat, touching the chair with a hand on the way down to help him judge the distance. "Thank you, sir. It's good to see you, too. Thanks for sparing the time."

"How've you been? Any improvement?" Ziehring's lean face was pulled even longer with concern, his green eyes scanning Noah's.

"The tinnitus is gone, for several months now."

"Well, that's good," he replied, the news lifting his pale-red eyebrows and brightening his features.

"Yes and no, sir. The ringing was driving me mad, but when it stopped, so did every other sound in that ear," he added with a gesture toward his left ear.

Ziehring frowned. "Ah. Is it permanent?"

"Seems to be so, sir." Noah swallowed thickly.

"And the blindness?"

"They're not sure. There's a chance I could recover some vision."

"A chance," Ziehring repeated.

"Yes, sir." Noah kept his voice calm, confident, unemotional. He didn't want Ziehring to think he was here to beg.

Captain took a deep breath, letting it out in a sigh, seeming to nod to himself. "Listen, Harkham," he began after a short silence, "no one would love to see you back in action more than I would. Except yourself, of course. You're a good cop, one of the best detectives I've had in a long time..." His voice trailed off.

"But it's not going to happen."

Ziehring looked him in the eye. "No, Noah. I don't think it is."

Noah looked away, angry and disappointed. Ziehring quickly continued, "No one is saying you can't come back, Harkham. Just that you can't be on the street. We could use you here, maybe in Dispatch–"

"Do you really think I could drive a desk the rest of my career?" Noah snapped. He realized that the volume of his voice was too loud, something he had to consciously control more now, and he reigned it in a bit. "I could do this, sir. I could be out there, doing my job, just like I always have."

He leaned forward, his hands on the front of Ziehring's desk, almost knocking over his brass nameplate. "Give me a chance to prove it."

But then he felt something cold and metallic press against his head, just above his left ear. He froze.

"If that had happened on the street, you'd be dead already," Ziehring looked apologetic but unwavering. "I'm sorry, Noah." He then nodded to the person behind him.

"I'm sorry, Hark," came a familiar voice.

Noah turned around to see Frankie putting away his gun, the Glock 17 he had used to protect Noah's back on the job now being used to stab him in it, so to speak. His former partner looked defeated, just as Noah himself felt. He looked to the corner left of the doorway and saw a chair positioned next to the large upright flag, in a slight shadow. Frankie had sat there the whole time, waiting for some signal from Ziehring. Waiting to humiliate him.

"Yeah," Noah replied, his voice quiet, defeated. "Yeah, me too, Frankie." He got up and exited the office.

Halfway down the hall he heard Frankie behind him, calling his name and catching him up. Noah stopped, then slowly turned around.

"Hark, I'm sorry," he said. "I wanted you to sense me coming. I really did."

"And what if I had? Ziehring already had his mind made up. You heard what he said."

"It was a last test. He wanted to be sure. If you could've somehow known I was there..."

"How? Huh?" He threw his hands up. "Ziehring's right. I had no right coming back here. I don't know what I was thinking, who I was trying to fool." He shook his head.

"Hark, don't, man," Frankie said, almost pleading.

"Just forget it," he said with a dismissive wave. "I'll see you around."

Frankie grabbed his arm as he started to walk away. "Wait. Just wait. The guys on the force, the newer guys, they're a bunch of cock-sure smartasses. They're all just 101s."

"That's how it's always been. So what?"

"Come back. Give them the benefit of your experience."

His brow furrowed. "What are you talking about?"

"Teaching, Hark. You didn't give the Captain a chance to talk about it, but – No, wait, think about it: you could teach seminars or something, tell them about the forensics stuff, train them to read the scene the way you can. The academy didn't make you the detective you are, your experiences did."

"You're serious."

"Yes. Don't let twelve years go to waste." He released his friend's arm as if he just realized he was still gripping it. "Just say you'll think about it."

Noah looked at him for a long moment, at the unrealistic hope in his friend's eyes. Could he do it? Could he settle for this? He turned away. "Take care of yourself, Frankie."

CHAPTER EIGHT

———

"A judge who cannot punish, in the end, associates themselves with the criminal."

Johann Wolfgang Von Goethe

"WE ARE CURRENTLY EXPLORING several avenues of inquiry and are confident we'll be making an arrest in due time," Detective Alan Franks announced into a cluster of microphones. He was standing in front of the precinct downtown, the sunlight giving the older, drab building an almost youthful glow. The wind ruffled the detective's short dark blond hair, but made the flags flanking the doors to the police station stand at attention.

"Detective," a reporter cut in, "what is the status of the victim, firefighter Vincent Perry?"

"I believe he's been upgraded to stable condition, but I don't have any further details than that."

"Any thoughts on who's responsible?"

"We are processing the evidence taken from the scene. It will take a little time, but I'm confident it will lead us to the perpetrator."

"Detective!" Several reporters shouted at the same time. The cop gestured to one older gentleman, who asked, "Do you have any idea why Firehouse Twelve was targeted?"

"I can't answer that question at this time. I'm sorry, no further questions."

He clicked off the television, silencing the babbling chatter of reporters. It was the same clip they'd been running all afternoon. He'd watched it five times already, each time refusing to believe what his eyes and ears were telling him.

He had failed.

Which meant he had to try again. But it was far too risky to go back to the fire station. They would be too alert now, watchful. He would have to target someone else. Someone else entirely. The police had only bothered to involve a few of its finest: two detectives and a handful of officers. It would be too personal to go after one of them; he would have to know their names, see their faces. Best to avoid that as long as possible. But the whole hospital had been involved. The personnel there was larger.

He just had to figure out how to do it. To do it cleanly and impersonally. And this time, he couldn't fail.

CHAPTER NINE

———

"THE BULLET IS A .38 semi-jacketed soft point. It has six grooves and a left-hand twist, which narrows it down to a Colt or Mirok .38 Special used to fire it," Robin "Shots" Dorian dictated into her tape recorder. She paused, thinking, a deep frown-induced furrow creasing her forehead. "The bullet weight is 110 grains," she continued, but paused again as memory tugged at her thoughts. She ran one hand through her thick brown hair then massaged the back of her neck and shoulder.

She switched off the tape recorder and stared at the bullet, trying to grasp the annoying memory flitting just out of reach in her mind. Something about those specs was troubling her. She could almost have sworn she had dictated the very same thing before. Like déjà-vu. Granted, .38 Specials were popular in the area, but something told her it was more than that.

Neil Coates tapped on the door and entered, startling her. "Sorry," he apologized, seeing her reaction, "didn't mean to scare you. Is this a bad time?" He regarded her with those still, grey-blue eyes.

"No," she said with a sheepish laugh, "I was just thinking, is all. What's up?"

"I was just hoping to get whatever you can give me on the bullet and casing from the fire station shooting. Whatever you got, you know, I want to show Cal what progress we've made."

"A bone to appease the slavering hounds," she said. "I haven't gotten anything official written up yet, but I can make you a copy of my prelim."

"Thanks," he said, gazing around the ballistics lab while he waited for her to make the copy. "I don't think I've ever told you, but I like what you've done with the place."

"Really?" Robin said, looking at him from the nook between her office and the day-shift tech's where the copier and fax machines sat. "It's not much different than it was when I got here." She sat the preliminary report on the copier's glass and had to press the button twice before it spat out a copy. She brought it back out, wiping some stray specks of toner off the edges of the paper.

A ghost of a grin tugged at his lips. "O'Brien had these cheesy public service announcement-type posters on the front and everything was arranged with slide-rule precision."

He made a gesture indicating the long metal counter where she had been examining the bullet next to the IBIS terminal, the other countertops where an array of different microscopes stood like toy soldiers, the cabinets containing her other equipment and the desk where her desktop computer sat on the stained oak tabletop. "This layout makes more sense."

"Wow, I thought that guy looked like a nerd," she handed him the copy of the report. "Most of us lab techs are, I know, but that guy?" She shook her head. "Yikes."

He gave a light chuckle. "Thanks," he said, lifting the report. "So what about you? You've never said what made you decide to don a lab coat for a living."

She glanced down at the white coat covering her simple yet flattering dress clothes underneath. "What? You don't think it completes the ensemble?"

This elicited a laugh. He turned to leave, giving her a parting nod. Deciding to take advantage of this rare open mood, she called out to him just before he got to the hall. "Hey, Neil?"

He ducked back in. "Yeah?"

"Listen, I heard about how they're going ahead with a formal inquiry – with the whole Turner case thing. I just want you to know I think it sucks. If there's anything I can do, don't hesitate, okay?"

"How did you hear about that?"

As usual, she couldn't tell by his expression if he was angry or not, or if she should have just kept her big mouth shut. "I ran into Ward at the beginning of the shift," she said cautiously. "He mentioned it, said he was upset they couldn't just let it go. Hey, you know, forget I said anything. I'm sorry – it isn't my place to bring it up, and, you know, not like you want to be reminded, right?"

"No, it's okay. Really. I just thought maybe one of the higher ups let something slip I didn't already know. But thanks for the offer, though I think I need divine intervention to get this whole thing sorted out."

She reached up and pulled a delicate silver cross necklace from beneath her shirt. "Then I'll pray you get it."

"Thanks, Shots," he said with genuine warmth.

She smiled. "Don't worry about it anyway. They're idiots if they believe that guy's story over you."

His pager beeped. "That's Parker," he said after reading the screen. "I'll see you later?" He sounded apologetic he had to leave so soon.

"Yeah, you bet," Robin said with a smile. He nodded and left the lab, heading in the direction of the conference room. Though he was out of sight, she still found herself smiling. She chuckled self-consciously and got back to work.

CHAPTER TEN

NEIL NOTICED ROBIN's fingerprint in toner ink on the middle left of the report as he was reading it over on the way to the conference room. He ran his thumb over it, but it didn't come off. He smiled.

"Hey, man," Conrad said, meeting up with him in the hallway. "Is that the ballistics report?"

He looked up from the page. "Preliminary report. Shots is still processing, but she's given us everything she's got so far," he said, handing over the report.

".38 Special," he read aloud. "There's a lot of those in this city." He handed it back. "But, maybe we'll get lucky and get a hit off IBIS."

They entered the small conference room. Parker sat at the wood veneer table, holding a length of navy blue rope patterned with spiraling red stripes. "MonTech medium-weight nylon mountain climbing rope," he announced as they sat down. "It's a soft-handed rope with just enough texture to give a good grip while climbing without being too rough on the palms. It can support up to 550 pounds – and it is the type of rope our shooter used to get in through the fire station window."

"So we're looking for a mountain climber?" Conrad asked. "Riverdale isn't exactly the Rockies – what would anyone around here be doing with mountain climbing gear?"

"That's a good question," Parker replied. "Maybe he does it on vacation."

"There are indoor climbing walls," Neil added. "The campus has one in its rec center. There's another at the SunGold downtown. I've been a few times; they use similar rope, if I remember right."

Parker smiled, his thin lips stretching like a longbow. "Then guess where you get to go today. But after we talk ballistics."

"The bullet recovered from Vincent Perry's chest was a .38 caliber," Neil reported. "Shots says the rifling narrows it down to three gun types: Colt .38 Special, Mirok .38 Special, or a Colt .357 Magnum. She's still working on the casing, but the preliminary report says she doesn't think it's going to tell us very much beyond the brand name – Wildcat – which we already knew. They're a smaller manufacturer based in Wisconsin; they've got several distributors across the country, one of which is here in town. I checked with them yesterday and they're faxing over a list of customers who purchased that brand and caliber within the last year."

"Excellent. Then we can try to cross-reference it against registered owners of Colts or Miroks in the area and run the bullet through IBIS. Any progress on the message?"

Neil shook his head. "Generic permanent marker you can get from any store, anywhere. Foster's looking at the handwriting, but he says since it was on a vertical surface and probably written very quickly, it won't likely be a true representation of the shooter's usual handwriting. And no prints or DNA on the cap. It's all a dead end."

Parker frowned. "Perhaps, but we can't discount the message out of hand entirely...Conrad, where are we on the shoeprints?"

"The shoes are a size 10 ½ regular, brand name Kickz – with a z – style called the Skeet. They're sort of a knock-off of the good skater shoes."

"Skater shoes?" Parker repeated. "You mean we're looking for a kid?"

"Not necessarily. Back in California they were pretty popular with the thirty-something athletic types. Weekend surfers, basketball players, hockey guys...The guys just starting to feel too old to be young but still too young to be old."

"Mountain climbers? Or, at least, rock wall climbers? Why don't you go with Neil to check out the walls? Maybe our guy decided his workout at the fire station wasn't enough for one week."

Neil looked at his watch. "It's almost seven; we better get Frankie and get going before they close for the night."

NEIL, FRANKIE AND CONRAD decided to check out the SunGold first, since it was more widely used by the public. SunGold had originally been just a tanning salon, but when the adjacent laundromat went out of business, the owner of the salon bought and remodeled the space. Into the new addition, high tech gym and weight-training equipment had been installed.

About four years ago a segment of the rear of the building had been raised to the two-story level to accommodate the huge rock wall the facility was now famous for. The SunGold Fitness and Tanning Salon was now the highest grossing gym or fitness center in the city. There were rumors the owner was trying to buy out one of the two adjoining businesses to put in an Olympic-sized pool and sauna.

When the two CSIs and the detective told the SunGold's manager – a lean, hard-body named Jeff York – why they were there, he adopted an almost defensive posture. "You honestly think it might have been someone enrolled here?" He pointed to the floor with a lift of one eyebrow as if to say the idea was ludicrous.

They were in his office, Neil and Conrad seated in uncomfortable plastic chairs, Frankie standing by a set of lockers. York sat in the chair behind his cream-colored aluminum desk. The whole office seemed like a throwback to a high school gym teacher's office.

"It's a possibility," Frankie answered. "Though if he were smart, he wouldn't have a membership, he'd just pay for each individual visit. That way, there'd be no paperwork linking him to this place."

York seemed relieved by that prospect, the exact opposite of how the other three felt. "If that's the case, how can I possibly be of help? I can't run a background check on everyone who walks through the door."

"Mr. York, you seem somewhat less than enthusiastic to help us out," Frankie observed. "We haven't accused you of any involve –"

"I didn't have anything to do with this!"

"That's what I'm saying, Mr. York. So forgive me for being confused, but I would think you'd be only too happy to assist us in ruling out your facility as the source of the climbing gear used in this crime." He gave the man an innocent, friendly expression.

York sighed, crossing his arms. "What do you need?"

"A list of your enrolled members and for you to check your gear for the rock wall, see if any of it is missing," Frankie replied.

"Shouldn't take but a few minutes of your time, Mr. York," Conrad assured him.

"All right," York said. "But what happens if something is missing?"

"Ah, I wouldn't worry about that until we need to, right, Neil?" Conrad said, getting to his feet with a tap on his partner's shoulder.

"Right. Worrying is bad for the soul," Neil answered dryly.

York led them through the maze of stair-climbers, ellipticals and treadmills toward the rear of the gym. Here the nine-foot ceiling vaulted to twenty, all of which was taken up by a very intimidating rock wall some twenty feet wide. At the moment, a fit blonde was making her way up a simulated chimney – a cleft in the rock face where the two sides are close enough together a climber can wedge in between and ascend. Along one wall flanking the synthetic stone was a large cabinet secured with a hefty padlock. York withdrew a cluttered ring of keys from his pocket, selected a small one and used it to open the cabinet.

Inside the cabinet was an array of harnesses and ropes, gloves for improved gripping, helmets and pads, some replacement toe and hand holds and spare parts for the climbing gear. On the inside of the door was a laminated inventory list. "This list is updated weekly, even if there are no changes to record," York explained. "Every piece of equipment is counted and logged, and the list is laminated to prevent tampering."

"Why all the security measures?" Neil asked.

"This equipment is top of the line. We just want to make sure no one mistakes the rental for a long-term lease, if you get me."

"Right. So who else besides you has a key to the cabinet?" Frankie asked.

"Just the wall managers. I have two employees exclusively in charge of the wall. There are usually three or four other employees who will help out here as well – getting people harnessed up, helping monitor safety, that sort of thing. But they don't have access to the storage locker. And before you ask, the wall's night supervisor is that dark-haired guy instructing the blonde climber. His name is Brian Hughes and you can ask him whatever you want to when he's finished helping her. Meanwhile, I'm guessing you'll want me to do a thorough inventory check."

"Yes, please," Frankie said with a genteel smile.

Conrad, meanwhile, was watching the blonde. "Take whatever time you need." He watched a long moment, then said, "Hey, Coates, you said you've climbed this thing?"

"Yeah, a couple of times. Why – you thinking of trying it?"

"I don't know, maybe. Looks kinda fun."

"Come with me next time, I'll show you how it's done. I can't believe you've never been rock wall climbing. I thought you were Mr. Outdoor-extreme-adrenaline-junkie."

"I am. I just don't do well with heights, you know? I'm not afraid or anything, I just get sort of disoriented. Like vertigo, I guess."

"The key is to not look down," York offered. "If you focus on the rock face, on the holds, you won't have time for vertigo, you'll be too distracted... Wait," he paused and frowned, perplexed. "That can't be right. Hey, Brian?"

The night supervisor looked over his shoulder at them. "Yeah, boss?"

"What setup is that?"

"Harness six. Why?"

"I can't find harness ten," York replied. "Do you know where it is?"

"It needs repaired, but Scott's better at that than me, so I left it and a repair request in a box in the cabinet for him a couple days ago. Maybe he hasn't finished with it yet."

"Maybe. But it should still be here."

Brain shrugged. "Give him a call."

"What brand of rope does harness ten have, Mr. York?" Neil asked.

York consulted the list. "Uhh...MonTech."

Neil and Conrad exchanged a look. "Maybe you should start worrying just a little bit now, Mr. York," Neil told him.

York contacted Scott Hughes, the wall's day supervisor, and was informed Scott had brought the broken set up home after his shift the previous day to repair it in his spare time. "He says it's in his garage," York reported.

"Ask him to just make sure it's still there, would you?" Frankie asked.

"Hey, Scott – do you think you could just check if it's still out there for me?" He listened a moment. "It's just a routine check – part of some investigation. It's no big deal, we just have to verify the location of our equipment for 'em."

A moment passed. "He's checking," York updated them. Then, apparently, Scott said something York didn't expect. "You what?" York asked, the color draining from his face. "Oh no," York said, looking sick to his stomach. "He says – he can't seem –"

"It's not there," Frankie supplied. "Tell him not to touch anything. We'll be right there. Where does he live?"

Conrad speed-dialed Parker while his partner got the address. "Cal – I think we've got a lead on the climbing gear...Yeah, we're on our way to check it out now. We'll let you know what we find."

CHAPTER ELEVEN

———

"To sin by silence, when they should protest, makes cowards of men."

-Ella Wheeler Wilcox

NO TIME TO LOSE. HE slipped on the scrubs he'd bought earlier that day. They weren't the standard green ones most doctors wore, but the more colorful ones close to the ones he'd seen some nurses wearing. They weren't exact, but they should at least get him in the door.

He snapped on a cheap pair of latex gloves and opened the package containing the new tools he'd bought just for this project. After removing every tag that could identify where the tools had come from, he placed them into a small paper bag that he would carry in as if it were his lunch. He brought to mind the layout of the hospital he'd memorized when he'd done recon a couple days ago. The best way to do this without getting caught was to wait for a trauma to come into the ER, slip in during the chaos, pull it off and slip back out.

He didn't have to wait long once he arrived at the hospital for a diversion. Two ambulances came wailing up to the entrance and were met by waiting teams of doctors and nurses, who slammed the gurneys through double doors with efficient urgency. He waited just a moment before trailing in after them. Everyone's attention was riveted on the newly-arrived patients, just as he had hoped. A swift perusal of the posted emergency evacuation route map confirmed the location of the nearest break-room.

He walked purposefully down the hall to where it was situated. A casual look through the partially closed blinds on the windowed door showed a solitary doctor occupying it, but she was heading toward the door. He waited just past the door as the doctor exited, then slipped into the break-room in her wake. It only took a moment to select his target and set to work.

A short time later he slipped back into the hall leading to the crowded lobby, where he disposed of the gloves in a bin full of others the doctors had used and thrown away. The paper bag had been thrown away in the break-room, with dozens just like it. After weaving through a small knot of people waiting to be treated for minor complaints, he exited through the double doors and began to walk slowly, naturally, down the street.

Ducking into an empty side street, he paused long enough to strip off the scrubs he had worn over his own clothes. He tossed them into a rusty metal trashcan along with the tools and set them on fire with the lighter he always carried with him. He watched just long enough to make sure the fire did its job, but nowhere near as long as he wanted. Then, satisfied with the result, he emerged from the side street, entered the busy thoroughfare and blended into the crowd to disappear.

CHAPTER TWELVE

"HEY, DOCTOR CHARLES," Amy Simpson greeted the resident with a grin.

"Hi, Amy," he replied with a distracted smile. They were in the break room just off the ER nurse's station, and he was looking over a thick notebook filled with his small, precise handwriting. He knew this precision would fall by the wayside once he was seeing dozens of patients each day on his own, but for now he prided himself on his legibility - especially since all the nurses had complimented him on it.

He looked up at her for a moment. "Thanks for saving my neck with that patient earlier – if you hadn't reminded me he was diabetic..." he shook his head at the thought.

"No problem, that's what we're here for," she replied, crossing over to the industrial sized coffee machine on the counter. She stepped down and he heard a small plash. Looking up he saw she had stepped in a small puddle of coffee. "Ugh," she sighed.

"Oh, sorry," Doctor Charles said, getting up. "I thought I got it all up. I spilled some coffee when I poured my cup."

"When you poured the last cup, doctor," she said with mock severity.

He flushed a bit. "Here, let me clean that up for you," he said, reaching for some paper towels. "Sorry, I'm not really familiar with the machine yet. I managed to put in the coffee and filter but – I was hoping someone would show me how to get it to ..." he made a vague gesture with both hands.

"It's all right, you just have to flip this switch." She pushed the button to get the machine to brew another pot. But instead of the sound of the internal carafe filling up with water, they heard a crackling. "That's strange-"

Before she could say more, a bright flash of light went off with a small popping sound behind the machine. This was followed by tall flames, which then spread to a pile of napkins and paper cups that had been set too near it.

"Whoa!" Dr. Charles cried out and frantically looked for something to put the fire out with. He spied the fire extinguisher on the wall and grabbed it. "Stand back!"

He doused the flames and then they both just stood there, shocked by the unexpectedness and intensity of the fire. "What in the world just happened?" he asked her.

She shook her head, trembling all over. "I don't-" she stopped mid-sentence, her breath wheezing as she clutched at her left arm.

"Amy?" Doctor Charles asked, brows furrowed. "Oh my - Amy!" he said, realizing what was happening. He tried to grab her to help her sit but her body crumpled to the floor before he could. He dropped to kneel beside her and checked her vitals. Her heart stuttered to a stop beneath his fingertips.

"Come on, Amy," he coaxed, pumping her chest. He forced air into her lungs and felt for a pulse again. He jumped up and tore open the door. "I need a crash cart in here!" he yelled to the nearest medical professional, who happened to be his attending, Doctor Cooke.

Cooke sprang into action, calling out orders at the nurses around her. She followed Charles into the break room and gasped when she saw Amy lying on the floor.

"What happened?" Cooke asked, going to the unconscious nurse and, after assessing her condition, taking over CPR. Charles just stared down at the nurse who had just a few moments ago been chatting pleasantly with him; the nurse who had saved his career only a few hours ago. "Doctor Charles! What happened?"

"I don't know," he stammered. "I think – I think she had a heart attack."

"Damn it!" Cooke said, feeling for a pulse. "I think she's in V-Fib."

"Doctor Cooke," a nurse said as she entered with the crash cart, "I've got the – Amy?"

"Julie! Charge to 200!" Doctor Cooke ordered the stunned nurse. Doctor Charles pushed her aside and handed the paddles to Doctor Cooke.

"Charging to 200," he announced.

"Clear!" Doctor Cooke commanded, then, making sure everyone was clear, sent a jolt of electricity to the unconscious nurses' heart. Doctor Charles could only stand by, hoping it would start beating once more.

CHAPTER THIRTEEN

———

SHOTS RUBBED HER TIRED eyes with a thumb and forefinger and stretched. She had been staring at the computer screen for hours, searching her files for cases involving a Colt or Mirok with the right specs. She had been working at the lab for less than a year, but the number of cases she had worked on was already massive, and there were many .38s and .357s among them.

She took a break, deciding to go to the lounge for a cup of strong black tea, heavily sweetened and with a splash of milk – an old favorite and a sort of comfort food. She plopped a teabag into her large yellow ducky mug – a gift from her niece – and left the lab.

She found Parker in the lounge, frowning over a case file. "Hey, Bossa Nova, what's with the black cloud?" Shots asked, trying out another nickname for him.

That was one of her new hobbies, trying to pin nicknames on everyone she worked with after infamously earning her own in a darts tournament against Jake Saddler. He'd told her she had to drink a shot of whiskey every time she won a round, and since she doesn't drink, only got two down before deciding she couldn't take any more. She let her next throw send the dart to plunk into the seat of the chair Jake was sitting in, right between his legs. 'Guess I lose,' she'd said, and was dubbed 'Double shot Dorian,' which soon became just 'Shots,' from then on.

Parker glanced up over the top of the file. "Bossa Nova?" He considered it a moment. "A touch on the nose, maybe, but I like it. And to answer your question, I'm reviewing the Turner case. The board is sending someone from Special Services to look into Neil on Monday."

"I heard. Ward told me yesterday." She poured a lot more sugar than
was healthy into the mug. "The whole thing is bunk." She expected him
to agree and was concerned when all he did was give a noncommittal
'hmm.' She turned to face him. "Wait – what's that supposed to mean?
You're on his side, right?"

"I'm on the side of truth, of fact. Do I believe he's guilty? No. Can
I prove it? Not conclusively. Will it be enough to clear him?" He
shrugged.

"Oh no, Cal – he's not going to lose his job, is he?"

"I honestly don't know, Robin. If they agree to polygraph him, and if he
passes, then he should be fine."

"*If* he passes?" She arched an eyebrow at him. "Why wouldn't they agree
to polygraph him?"

"Ashton thinks they're old-fashioned and unreliable. He thinks they
can be interpreted too loosely, that nervousness or stress skews the
results. Or they can be manipulated. And to a degree he's right, but a
clear polygraph will at least throw doubt on Turner's accusations."

"You would think the fact the guy is accused of burning down a
building, killing dozens of people would have put a big enough dent in
his credibility."

His cell phone rang. "You would think," he said, then answered his
phone. "Parker." He was silent a long moment. "We'll be right there." He
hung up and then speed-dialed a number.

"What is it?" Robin asked.

He held up a finger. "Conrad, it's Parker. Grab your kit and meet me at the car –we have to get to the hospital. Near as I can make out, someone rigged the break room coffee maker to catch fire when someone flipped its switch." He listened, and then answered, "One nurse, they're working on her but they're not sure if she'll make it." He paused again then murmured a quick "okay" before hanging up.

Robin had just been reaching for the switch on their own industrial coffee maker to make it dispense hot water when Parker made this announcement and was now scrutinizing the machine. "Clever," she said admiringly.

"That's what worries me," he said as he exited.

She filled her mug, grabbed a spoon and stirred in some milk, and then noticed Parker had left the Turner file behind. She started to close the file and take it to his office, when something caught her eye. She frowned at the address of the building Turner was accused of torching, the same unidentifiable shock of recognition tingling the base of her skull.

Something suddenly fell into place. Grabbing up the file and her ducky mug, she rushed back to the ballistics lab.

"No way," she breathed when the computer screen confirmed her suspicion.

CHAPTER FOURTEEN

———

"FREAKIN' BRILLIANT," Conrad said as he examined the coffee machine, the back panel of which had been removed to expose the full extent of the tampering done to the wiring. The coating had been stripped back on the wires to the brew switch, and the char line on the inside of the panel indicated some sort of accelerant had been used to start the fire that then traveled to the outside of the machine, where it was fed by a pile of napkins and paper cups. Judging from the statement Dr. Charles gave, he guessed the accelerant had been flash powder or something similar.

"Yes," Parker agreed, eyeing the set up. Neither of them were closer than a few feet from the counter, keeping out of the puddle of water that had spewed out of the half-melted machine.

Parker proceeded to lay out a sheet of electrostatic lifting film and processed the area around the door into the lounge. As they both expected, several overlapping prints developed, and none too clearly. The area just in front of the machine would have been the best place to get the saboteur's shoe prints, but the spilled coffee, water and extinguisher foam had ruined their chances. To be thorough, however, he processed several areas of the floor while Conrad dusted for prints.

"There's gotta be a hundred prints on this thing," Conrad complained, dusting the break-room's door handle.

"Probably," Parker replied. "There are ten doctors on the ER staff and eight nurses. And five med students. Who knows how many times a day each one comes in here?"

"Thanks, Boss," Conrad said wryly. "Okay, so only twenty-three people to try to sort through, that's much better."

"And just think: this is a hospital, he probably snagged a pair of latex gloves on the way in," he smiled impishly.

"So I could be doing this for nothing. Oh well – I could always use the exercise in futility," he grinned. He lifted the dusted prints, then pointed his camera toward the message scrawled on the wall behind the coffee maker. ...*Too late,* it read. "If he's gonna go to the trouble of leaving us messages, why can't he just tell us what his deal is?"

"No criminal is ever considerate enough to write a nice, neat note saying, 'Hi, my name is John Doe and I did this because fill in the blank.'"

"Why the frick not? All this creepy 'I'm the scary bad guy leaving obscure clues' crap is annoying," Conrad grumbled. He took a few more pictures, and then eyed the machine. "We ready to pack up this bad boy now?"

Parker handed the electrostatic films to Ward. "Yep. Hold these."

With that, he knelt down and reached under the little table to unplug the power strip. The appliances connected to it winked off. He emerged from the table and sat the power strip on top of it, pushing aside Styrofoam cups and packets of sugar and sweetener. They had already photographed the damage in situ when they arrived, but now that they had processed the floor and surrounding areas, they were able to start on the sabotaged machine.

"No way," Conrad said, examining one of the films. "Cal, check this out."

"No way?"

Conrad turned the film toward him and pointed at one particular print. "That's a Kickz Skeet," he said, "and I can't be sure, but it looks like it's a ten-and-a-half regular."

"Could be from one of the staff members," Parker cautioned, "or a med student. We'll have to rule all twenty-three out first."

A tingle of excitement coursed through him. "I know, but I'd bet my next paycheck that these are the same shoes that were at the fire station and in Scott Hughes' garage."

Parker's cell phone rang. "Dust that cord," he instructed Ward, then answered, "Parker." He moved to the other side of the room to get out of the way, but put the phone on speaker.

"Cal – I think I may be onto something," Robin Dorian announced on the other end of the line.

"Whatcha got, Robin?"

"Something about the specs for the .38 we pulled out of the fireman triggered a memory for me. Long story short I followed a hunch – I think someone should have a chat with Bobby Avalon."

"The boxer who injured Detective Harkham?" Parker asked in complete shock.

Conrad looked up at him, frowning curiously. "Avalon? Why?"

"Oh, hey there, Point Break," she said with a chuckle. "Yeah. Turns out he's one of the very few people known to have bought Wildcat brand .38 semi-jacketed soft-point ammunition in the last two years. Plus, the gun he had the day Harkham was injured was a Colt .357 Magnum – which discharged a Wildcat .38 bullet. He also has a Colt .38 special registered in his name."

"I'm starting to love your hunches, Robin," Parker said with a wide grin.

"Don't get too happy, Bossa Nova," she cautioned. "Avalon reported the .38 Special stolen a month before he was arrested."

"Interesting. Not that it means the gun was actually stolen."

"I know. And here's where it gets really interesting. The date it was reported stolen was the day before Simon Turner burned down the Brookview apartment building. And guess who was living in that building at the time?"

"Avalon," Conrad supplied, feeling everything falling into place.

"Bingo. And IBIS kicked out a bullet with identical specs recovered from an armed robbery case about the same time. A string of convenience stores were knocked over the night before the Turner arson. The armed robbery was never solved, but the gun used in it was the same gun used to shoot Vincent Perry."

"Incredible," Parker muttered. "But why didn't anyone connect Avalon to the robberies?"

"Well, he was questioned, but he denied any involvement, of course –"

"Of course."

"But the gun was never found and without that exemplar, there was no way to prove it was his Colt used in the robbery. But I think it's time he was paid another visit."

"Excellent, excellent work, Robin. I'll call Franks and see to it once we're finished here."

"Thanks, boss. What's the word on the nurse? Will she make it, d'you think?"

"It's hard to say at this point. She had a heart attack from the shock of the fire – no one's saying anything more than that. She was very fortunate someone else was there when it happened."

"Yeah, she was. Thank God it wasn't as bad as it could have been. Anyway, you're busy – just let me know how it goes with Avalon, okay?"

"Definitely. Thank you, Robin."

"You bet."

"No way," Conrad said once she'd hung up. "Freak cosmic coincidence? I mean, what are the odds?"

CHAPTER FIFTEEN

———

FRANKIE AND NEIL COATES sat across the interrogation room table from Jason Campbell, a semi-regular at the SunGold and a former guest at county lock-up courtesy of a grand larceny indictment. He was also known to be a former 'acquaintance' of known violent offenders and other delinquents. A coincidence neither the cop nor the criminalist found insignificant.

"Mr. Campbell, you have a membership at SunGold, isn't that right?" Frankie asked the ex-con.

"That's right." He was a thin man with a lean, toned frame. He reminded Frankie of a young Frank Sinatra – if old Blue Eyes had been more into bench presses than microphones.

"And you served a year in county for stealing a few hundred dollars' worth of jewels from your girlfriend's mother, correct?"

"Nah, she wasn't my girl, she was just a waitress I knew through a mutual friend. And she hired me to do it – said she had been cut off by the old bat and was sick of livin' off tips. Said she'd split the money fifty-fifty and be very grateful for my help, if you get my meaning." He leered, then his expression clouded. "She also said nobody'd be home. She was wrong."

"How long have you been out?"

"Six months. What's with all these questions? That stuff's all in my file, which you have right in front of you. I thought we were gonna be talking about some of my former associates."

"Okay," Frankie said, "let's talk about the guys you used to hang with. When was the last time you spoke to Trevor Angelo?"

"I haven't seen or spoken to Angelo since before I went away."

"Really?" Frankie said, raising his eyebrows. "Well, that's interesting because Mr. Angelo also has a membership at SunGold."

"That is interesting," Campbell said. "Small world."

"Yes, indeed," Frankie muttered.

"Do you like to climb the rock wall over SunGold," Neil asked, changing course.

"Yeah. So what?" Campbell crossed one foot over his other knee and jiggled it, his eyes wary.

"Hey, nothing, man – I climb it once in a while myself. But I find it's not much of a challenge unless you're, say, three stories off the ground. What do you think?"

"I guess, I don't know," he replied, a little confused. "Whatever. Are we done here?"

"Not quite," Neil cut in before Frankie could answer. "What size shoe do you wear?"

"Ten. Why?"

"Ten, hmmm. See, that's also interesting because the bottom of those All-Stars you're wearing say you wear a 10 ½."

"These run a little small. You wear a ten, you buy a ten point five in these."

"A friend of mine used to have shoes like those," Neil continued, his placid expression giving nothing away. "He liked to skate back in college. Only he sank all his money into his board and his half-pipes so he couldn't afford the good shoes. He got those knock-offs they call Kickz. You know which ones I'm talking about?"

"Yeah, I seen 'em before."

"You ever buy any?" Frankie asked.

"Hell no. Those things are cheap for a reason, man. They ain't worth crap."

"Which harness do you use when you climb?" Neil asked, changing tack again.

"Whichever one they give me," he replied after the slightest pause, in which he looked like he was trying to get a sense of the trap that was being set for him.

"They usually try to match up certain setups to each member. See, they have different sizes, different weight capacities. They give me number seven or eight whenever I'm there."

"I guess I just never paid attention."

"According to Mr. York's records – he's the guy who owns SunGold, by the way," Frankie told him, "they like to make notes for repeat customers, keep track of equipment preferences and so on. His records indicate both you and Mr. Angelo often used harness ten. It really is a small world after all."

"Look, I don't know what any of this has to do with anything. I served my time, I went straight and I haven't had any contact with any of the old crew since I been out. Check with my parole officer. I have a legitimate job, my own place and I'm whipping myself into shape at the gym. If you're trying to accuse me of something, then I want my lawyer here."

"Hey, if you can tell us where you were around four o'clock this afternoon and around twelve-thirty last Sunday night, you can walk right on out of here with our fare-thee-well," Frankie said.

"I was working at the lumber yard from nine a.m. to five p.m. today. Sunday night I was at my apartment all night."

"Can anyone verify that?"

"Yeah, my landlord. He's got my place monitored. You know, camera in the hall outside my front door, bars on the windows. The whole building is on lock-down after ten p.m." He looked at them like this was all supposed to be familiar to them. "It's housing for ex-cons and parolees, like a half-way house. Almost like I never left prison."

———————

"ALL RIGHT," NEIL SAID out in the hall after Campbell left. "What now?"

"I liked Campbell for this," Frankie said, running a hand through his short dark-blonde hair. "He seems the type. I know Trevor Angelo, he's strictly small-time, nickel and dime stuff. No way he's smart enough to have pulled this off."

"Campbell is no genius either," Neil said, "but there's a possibility that the two are working together. Campbell pulling the strings. Or they're just doing the heavy lifting for someone else. But even that theory begs the question of why these victims? What would a fire fighter and a nurse have to do with two ex-cons?"

"I don't know," he sighed. "It's not like our guy could have predicted who was going to flip the switch, so he wasn't going after Amy Simpson specifically...and looks like he only shot Vincent Perry because he caught him fleeing the firehouse. So what we need to know is: what's the connection between Firehouse Twelve and Bell Memorial Hospital?"

"Yeah...I don't know. I think I'll check in with Parker – I haven't seen him in a few hours, maybe he got something that'll help answer that question."

"All right. I'll talk to Trevor Angelo, just to be thorough, though I doubt there's any possibility he was involved." The two went their separate ways and, as Frankie got to his car, his cell phone rang. "Franks," he answered. He listened while Parker filled him in on the evidence recovered from the scene.

"Conrad recovered a plain brown paper bag from the hospital lounge trash that had part of the cardboard backing from what looks like a blister package for a pair of pliers or wire strippers. There was no receipt or the rest of the package, but there was a partial price tag – it's pretty faint; we're taking it back to the lab to process it."

"Great work, both of you. Anything else?"

"Yeah, there's one more thing." Parker proceeded to tell him about Robin's lead.

"Avalon?" he asked, incredulous.

CHAPTER SIXTEEN

———

"HEY, CAL — I THOUGHT you'd be back at the lab by now," Neil said when he finally got his boss on the line. "Are you still at the hospital?" Parker's phone had been going to voicemail for the past five minutes straight.

"No, Conrad and I finished up there a little while ago. We're following up a possible lead."

"Oh yeah? What did you find?"

"I think I'll see if there's any substance to it first," Parker replied evasively. "It could just be a dead end."

"Yeah, that's what Jason Campbell turned out to be."

"Who?"

"Jason Campbell: a would-be professional thief – if he didn't suck at it, that is. He's an ex-con with a membership at SunGold. He's used harness ten several times in the past and sometimes wears a size ten-and-a-half shoe. But his alibi checks out, Frankie just verified. We're going to check out another guy, Trevor Angelo-"

"Don't waste your time with Angelo, Neil. I know him: he's a drug mule who gets paid in a cut of the cargo. He's only got a couple of brain cells left and they never seem able to work together long enough to form a complete thought. What made you two look at him?"

"He's got a membership at SunGold and used the same harness at least once this past month. I figured him for a dead end, too, but we thought we should check him out anyway. Wouldn't want anyone to accuse us of not following protocol," he added, wryly.

"Speaking of, I've been meaning to talk to you," Parker said, his tone guarded. "I think Ashton is getting pressured to have you take yourself off the clock until this is all over."

"If I do that, I look guilty. If I just do my job, they'll see what kind of criminalist I am. I did nothing wrong, I'm not going to let them treat me like a criminal."

"It's just some friendly advice, Neil, but I think you shouldn't fight the Powers That Be on this. You've accrued a lot of vacation time, I think you should consider taking it."

"What's going on?" A knot was tightening in his chest. "Do you know something I don't?"

"All I can say is that Ashton was surprised and concerned I let you run primary on the fire scene. I assured him I did it because you are my best CSI for arson cases and had earned it. He thinks I should have made you take a backseat for the sake of appearances."

"Fine. Thanks for backing me, Cal, but I'm not going to let this mess spill over onto you. I'll step aside," it galled him to agree, but it was probably best, if it kept the rest of the lab clean.

"It's going to work out, Neil. Listen, I need to get off here, I'll see you later, okay?"

"Okay. I'll hand over all my reports. I'll leave them on your desk."

"Okay, great," Parker said as he hung up.

CHAPTER SEVENTEEN

———

BEFORE THEM – CONRAD, Parker and Frankie – was the seedy hotel where Bobby Avalon was residing. Because of a technicality and a jury that was somehow won over by Avalon's attorney, Avalon had gotten off with only a few minor charges. He paid some heavy fines and served eight months of a one year sentence, getting off early for good behavior. Prison records showed he'd been released three weeks ago.

His former girlfriend – the one who had called the cops on him that day – had filed a restraining order and threw all his belongings out of the window of their apartment. She moved, leaving no forwarding address and the super changed the locks on the apartment and re-rented it within a week. Avalon had ended up at this fleabag hotel and had been there ever since.

And now a cop and two criminalists were knocking on his door.

"Bobby Avalon- Cal Parker and Conrad Ward with the Calera County Crime Lab," Parker announced through the closed door. "We need to speak with you. We're here with -"

"Go away," came a gruff reply. "You're not cops – I don't have to let you in."

"They aren't cops, Mr. Avalon," Frankie replied, "but I am. Detective Franks, Riverdale Police Department. If you make me come back with a warrant, you'll not only have to open the door, you'll have to come to the station while these two toss your apartment. We just need some information. I don't know about you, but I'd rather discuss things here." He was clenching his fists, a tightness in his posture that looked ready to unleash at any second.

A moment passed. Then, with a clunk, Avalon drew back the deadbolt, unlocked the handle and opened the door. He was wearing a tee shirt that had once been white but was now a dingy ecru and boxing trunks – the loose-fitting nylon kind he wore in the ring. But one glance at the man told them it had been quite some time since Bobby "The Mallet" Avalon had set foot beyond the ropes. He squinted at the badge Frankie held up for inspection. "All right, what do you want?" Avalon stood holding the door, blocking their entry.

"May we come in?"

Avalon sniffed derisively, then stood aside and welcomed them in with an exaggerated, grand sweep of his arm. "Sure. Make yourselves at home. Can I offer you a cocktail, perhaps some caviar?" He sneered at his own sarcasm.

Parker, Conrad and Frankie entered the shabby 'suite' and scanned the place for any weapons Avalon might decide to use if he didn't like what he was hearing. All they could see, however, was clutter. Dirty clothes, takeout containers, crumpled magazines and beer cans littered every available surface.

"How about you just answer a few questions and we'll get out of your hair?" Parker answered, hesitating on the last word with a glance at Avalon's shaved head. Conrad suppressed a grin.

"All right, but make it quick. I'm supposed to be at the ring in an hour."

"So you still box?" Conrad asked.

"Sometimes. Mostly I instruct. I'm forty-three, I'm getting a little too old for the gloves. Are you gonna tell me why you're here?"

"Last year, just a month before you got arrested, you reported a Colt .38 Special stolen, is that right?" Frankie asked.

"Yeah. Did you find it or somethin'?"

"Do you have any idea who might have stolen your weapon?"

"Coulda been lots of people. Everyone I know knew about my guns. I owned 'em legal, and I let everyone know I had 'em, you know, to tell 'em nobody better mess with me. The kind of people I know, you had to let 'em know, you know?"

"Yeah, I get you," Conrad said. "And you were living in the Brookview apartment building then, right? So it was stolen the day before the apartment building went up in smoke, right?"

"That's right."

"And so you moved in with your girlfriend Talia after that, right?"

"Yeah. But I found out she had been layin' money against me and my fighters in the ring, makin' me look like a chump, you know? So, I got drunk and I slapped her around a little. I didn't really hurt her, though. I passed out and when I came to, she was gone. All I found was a note sayin' how she'd been having another fighter on the side and was through with me."

"And you were angry," Conrad added.

"You bet I was. And I was messed up, so I shot the couch. Next thing I know I got cops comin' at me from all directions." He smirked at them. "And, well, you know the rest of *that* story."

Frankie looked ready to take the boxer down. Conrad felt his own anger flare before he could rein it in. "Yeah, man. A good cop's career was ended by a two-bit has-been boxer. It's a shame the court couldn't sentence you to get what you gave him. But I guess it doesn't matter now, since the magnificent Mallet has been thrown on the garbage heap with the rest of the used-up tools."

"Excuse me?" Avalon got in his face.

"You heard me, man." He didn't back down, and could feel the adrenaline kicking in. "It shoulda been you who took that shot to the face or at the very least you should still be locked up -"

"Conrad," Parker warned, also laying a hand on Frankie's arm to restrain the livid cop.

Avalon's expression darkened. "I think it would be a very good idea for you to leave now."

"All right, Mr. Avalon," Parker said, "we'll go. But before we do, would you mind letting us see your shoe?"

"If it makes you leave, whatever." He took off one of his shoes and thrust it at Parker. "Knock yourself out."

Parker looked at the tag inside the malodorous footwear and handed it to Conrad. He looked inside: it was a size nine and a half. Frankie gave him a questioning glance, to which he responded with a negative shake of his head.

Frankie turned to Avalon, his fists clenched at his side. "If we were to ask you for a list of everyone who knew about your guns..."

Avalon tapped the side of his head. "I'd say a boxer's memory ain't too good. All them blows to the head, you know?" He glanced at Conrad and held out a hand. "My shoe?"

Conrad tossed it to him, hard, and followed Parker and Frankie out the door. "We done here?" Frankie asked them as they headed toward their vehicles.

"Yeah, Frankie, thanks," Parker answered.

Frankie nodded, fuming. "I can't believe - Dammit! I gotta get outta here and wash this scum off me." He got into his car. "You know how to reach me," he added in a leaden voice, speeding off.

Conrad got into Parker's car banged his fist on the dashboard. "Shit."

"Easy!" Parker said, getting in and putting his hands out to calm the younger man.

"I blew it, Cal. I lost my cool and screwed up the interview. I'm sorry." He was still pumped, a little shaky, and talking too loud.

"He wasn't going to give us what we wanted anyway. Don't beat yourself – or my car – up about it."

"He was so smug," he said, almost cutting Parker off. "It was like he was proud of what he'd done to Hark. I'm just glad Coates wasn't here," he fumed as Parker started the car and drove away.

"That's why I didn't tell him we were going to talk to the man who ended his cousin's career. That and the connection to Turner. If Ashton knew Turner's name had come up in this case and Neil knew about it, everything Neil has touched would be inadmissible."

"But now that he's on vacation..." he said, hating this kind of maneuvering just to get their jobs done.

"It should help assure the District Attorney that everything is kosher."

"Meanwhile, Neil gets to sit at home waiting to be interrogated like a criminal again," Conrad grumbled.

"Yes, but at least he's getting vacation pay. He could have been put on suspension pending investigation, without pay."

They fell silent a moment. Then Conrad said, "I don't see how anyone could believe he did anything wrong."

"I hate to say it, but if it had been any other crime, anything other than arson, the whole idea would have been immediately discarded as ludicrous."

"That's crap, Cal," Conrad said sharply. "That wasn't even a factor."

"You and I know that," he replied, "but to anyone on the outside, you have to admit it would throw up a red flag."

Conrad made a noncommittal grunt and they rode the rest of the way back to the lab in silence, each lost in thought.

CHAPTER EIGHTEEN

———

"HARKHAM," NOAH IDENTIFIED himself upon answering the phone - a habit left over from the job. He wiped a towel across his face and stepped off the treadmill in his bedroom, going to his fridge. The pitcher of ice water he sought was practically the only thing in there and he made a mental note to get to the store. Soon.

"Hark, it's Frankie."

"Hey. What's going on?" He kept his voice neutral.

"You sound out of breath, you okay?"

"Yeah, I'm fine. I just went for a run." He poured a glass of water and drank a long gulp.

"Good, that's...good. Listen, I was wondering if we could meet up. I feel lousy about being part of what happened in Ziehring's office. I want to make it up to you. Dinner anywhere you like, my treat."

"That's all right, Frankie. You don't have to do that. Besides, I'm glad it was you and not one of those smug-ass punks the academy is accepting these days." He hesitated a moment, wrestling with a decision. "What say I order a pizza from Gianni's and we just hang out here like we used to?"

"Sounds good," Frankie said, sounding relieved. "I'll bring the beer."

"You know I don't drink."

"Yeah, I know. I was just hoping to catch you off guard, that way if I brought 'em I could always say you told me it was okay."

Noah smiled. "It never worked in all these years, I don't think it's going to start working now."

He chuckled. "Worth a shot. I'll bring the usual. See you in a few."

"All right, man, be safe."

Twenty minutes later Frankie entered the apartment bearing the requisite film noir on DVD - this time it was *The Woman in the Window* - plus root beer for himself and ginger ale for his old partner. Noah had always been practically addicted to it, but Frankie couldn't stand it and always drank something else. The pizza guy showed up a few minutes after, delivering two large pizzas - one with everything except anchovies and olives, the other with just pepperoni, anchovies and extra cheese.

They planted themselves on Noah's couch - an off-white suede deal with a modern, almost airline lobby look to it - and Frankie started the movie. Noah twisted open a bottle of root beer and sat it next to Frankie's' plate on his granddad's old footlocker, which now served as his coffee table, then opened a bottle of ginger ale for himself. The routine feeling of it all was nice, familiar. Not everything in his life had changed because of Bobby Avalon.

"Just like the good old days, yeah?" Frankie asked, sucking down an anchovy and chasing it with root beer.

He chuckled. "Yeah, and that is still disgusting." He regarded his friend for a moment. "So, have you put in for Sergeant yet?"

"I've been thinking about it, but," he shrugged. "I'm not sure. I mean, it was different for you, you made Sergeant before making Detective..."

"I don't think we're all that different. Besides, they have a vacancy now," he added in an attempt to humorize his situation, trying to put him at ease. It backfired. Frankie winced and gave Noah a sidelong, uncomfortable look.

"Geez, Hark," he said, putting down his slice.

"What? If I can laugh about it, it shouldn't bother you to."

"Well, it does bother me. It sucks." He paused. "Besides, you ain't laughing."

"No. You're right, I'm not. Let's talk about something else. Tell me about the fire fighter and the nurse." He resumed eating his slice and spared a second's attention for Edward G. Robinson's plight playing out on his television screen.

"Okay. But I have to use hypotheticals, understand. I can't discuss specifics with you since you're not on the case."

"I remember," he grumbled, annoyed with the sour turn of the conversation. "How did the shooter get into the fire station without tripping the alarm? There was talk of an open window?"

To his credit, he didn't even ask how Noah was still so well informed. "Let's say, hypothetically, that the open window was on the third floor and the crime scene unit found synthetic fibers and gouges in the brickwork on the roof above the window. And there were shoeprints on the fire escape."

"That would suggest climbing gear: a rope and harness system, plus maybe a grappling hook or other anchoring device. So, what?, he goes up the fire escape to the roof, over to above the open window and rappels in? And since you didn't mention any of these hypothetical devices, their absence suggests he left the way he came: out the window to the roof and down the fire escape."

He paused the movie. "In this hypothetical crime scene, are there any surveillance cameras covering the fire escape and roof? Or the third floor itself?"

"None. The third floor is the sleeping quarters for crews pulling 24-hour shifts. The fire escape access had to be pulled down from about seven feet off the ground - he probably used his gear to help with that, too - so there aren't cameras on it directly. The ones that are in place cover the grounds around the entrances, the first floor and the second floor. Nobody saw a thing, and he avoided all of those cameras."

"Is there anything so far to indicate why the firehouse was targeted?"

Frankie swallowed a mouthful of root beer. "That's where it gets a bit murky. So far we can find nothing to link the two victims - or, I guess, the two buildings." He took another bite of pizza and chewed, lost in thought a moment. "For someone to sneak into a building and set a fire in a room full of sleeping people suggests the group of firefighters or one of them in particular was chosen specifically. But for someone to sneak into a hospital and juice up an appliance that any number of people might touch instead of planting, like an incendiary or something in a specific person's locker, for instance, suggests random, impersonal targeting. The two MOs seem to contradict each other."

"Maybe. But what if the fire was done the way it was because it was random?" Noah suggested, pointing his ginger ale toward Frankie with a raised eyebrow. "What if he didn't know who would be working that night? I mean, firefighters keep odd hours and shifts rotate in and out all the time. It seems to me he didn't have a specific target in mind, or else he would have set fire to their bed, or near it."

"But why that night? Doesn't that suggest his beef was with this particular group? I mean, it feels like if he wanted it to be random, he would have set the fire somewhere public. Targeting the firehouse dormitory seems purposeful. It takes the control out of Chance's or Fate's hands and puts it square into his."

"What if he doesn't believe in Chance or Fate? Then he becomes the sole controller of events, of life and death. It's like, say you see a bug. You can decide then and there whether or not you kill it. You control what happens to it. Now imagine a large group of insects - a colony of ants or something - and you decide to kill two of them, for some reason. Maybe you're a sadistic little kid with a magnifying glass. So you kill two of them, but without 'picking them out.' It's still random which ones die, yet the control over their lives was still in your hands."

"Randomly selected, yet still selected," Frankie paraphrased. "But what's his motive? A fire fighter, then a nurse." He thought a moment. "Maybe he's just targeting emergency personnel. Maybe he'll go after an EMT or something next. Or one of us." He glanced at him and amended, "A cop, I mean."

Noah chewed on the inside of his lower lip thoughtfully, trying to see the pattern. "Unless there is some method to it, something specific driving his choice of victims...Have you checked out fire-related fatalities? Ones in which the victims died at the hospital and not at the scene?"

"No," Frankie said, brightening. "No, we haven't yet."

"I think you'll want to check out surviving family members. Cross-referenced with those who have access to climbing gear. I presume you've already checked out facilities with climbing walls in the area for members with guns and/or criminal histories."

"Yes. Dead ends." He was looking at Noah with a pensive expression, but after a moment, turned away, his face unreadable.

"I'm used to it by now, Frankie, it's okay."

"What?" he said, snapping out of his musing.

"The scars. Everybody stares at them. I know you've tried not to, and I appreciate that, but I'm used to it now, so you don't have to worry about it."

"I wasn't meaning to, I was just...thinking."

"About?"

"Something I shouldn't have. Because now the thought won't go away, and I wish it would."

"Why is that?"

"Because I think I may be right."

"And you wish you weren't." Noah narrowed his eyes, considering this.

Frankie drained the dregs out of his bottle of root beer. "Yeah. I really do."

Noah turned more toward him. "What is it? What are you thinking?"

"I think...I shouldn't say anything until I'm sure."

"If you know something, a way to find and stop this guy - you better act fast, because he's failed to kill twice now. He'll try again, and I hate to think who his next target might be."

Frankie gave him an odd look. "Me too, Hark," he said.

CHAPTER NINETEEN

TUESDAY MORNING FOUND Detective Franks reviewing the Simon Turner-Brookview arson case. It was the most recent fatal fire in the area serviced by both the Bell Memorial Hospital and Firehouse 12. Almost two dozen people had died as a result of the arson - one as young as fifteen months and one as old as seventy-three years.

The mother of the fifteen month old had died in the hospital two days after the fire, so he added her boyfriend at the time of her death, as well as the infant's biological father, to his list of potential suspects. He looked into the families and associates of the eight other victims who had died at the hospital rather than at the scene, and added more names to the list. Once finished, he looked over the final list and sighed.

Twenty-six possibilities, if Hark's theory proved right. But he had to take Shots' angle into account, as well. Someone who had access to Bobby Avalon's Colt pistol and had lost someone in the fire. Someone who had been to the SunGold on the day Scott Hughes brought the broken harness home. Someone who wore a size 10.5 shoe. Find that person, and, well, case closed.

Frankie's gut told him both theories were true. That was the thought he'd had at Noah's apartment. And what made the thought so unpleasant was that he and Noah had worked the Brookview case, along with the uniformed officers who had been the first responders on the scene. They were probably next on this guy's list. And, since the attacks seemed indiscriminate, it could even mean that every cop was a potential victim. That was too large a pool to lifeguard; especially when he didn't know how or where the danger might come from.

He had no idea where to begin, so he began at the top of the list: the young mother's boyfriend. The guy – Joshua Wheeler – had no record or even so much as an outstanding parking ticket, but Frankie was able to pull up his driver's license and get a current address.

He looked at the long list of names and sighed. With any luck, Wheeler will be their guy and he would get this case wrapped up by dinner.

And Ziehring just might take up ballet.

An hour later he had run the names of everyone on the list for background checks, current addresses and current places of employment. Nobody stuck out as any more likely than the others, so he resigned himself to interviewing every single one, making for a long day of asking tough questions and receiving very little cooperation. He could find no excuse for any further delay, so set out to interrogate a bunch of grieving people who would resent any implication of guilt in these grisly crimes and the grim prospect he might be right about one of them.

———————————

"TO BE ABSOLUTELY HONEST, Detective, there were days when I could have done it." Joshua Wheeler made this confession within the confines of his dimly lit, closet-like office at New Hope Shelter, surrounded by barred windows and a counter that was separated from the lobby by thick metal fencing. The elements combined to give the space an atmosphere somewhere between that of a confessional and a prison. It was oddly appropriate.

"But instead you threw yourself into your work?" Frankie asked with a gesture taking in their surroundings.

"I had volunteered here for a credit back in college. After the fire I...I needed to do something that mattered." He shrugged his thin shoulders and Frankie noticed how everything about this guy was linear – long nose, straight eyebrows and mouth, close-trimmed straight brown hair and a thin, angular frame. "I was one of those guys who couldn't turn down overtime, you know, a workaholic. I was up for a promotion; three weeks away from becoming Head of Acquisitions – complete with executive office suite, new company car in the form of a BMW, and the key to the executive washroom. We were finally going to get out of that crappy apartment building. I was at work when I got the call."

He paused a moment to blink back tears and cleared his throat. "Sorry," he said, "I haven't gotten used to it yet."

"I understand. Take your time." Frankie found himself wondering how hard it would be to make yourself cry on command. A pang of shame for this callousness brought him up short. This man was a victim, after all, even if a potential suspect as well.

"Thank you, but I've got to talk about it now and then or it will eat me alive." His somber smile was more a grimace. "I was still at work at a quarter 'til ten when the phone rang. I figured it would be Julia calling to tell me to get my butt home...it was the police instead." He seemed to get lost in memory for a moment. "She came to, once, on the second day. I got to talk to her for just a moment before – I told her I loved her and then she was just gone.

"Our boy went quicker," he continued. "The smoke got to him, but he was a fighter. He made it to the ER," tears stood glistening in his eyes, but a sad smile tugged at his quivering lips.

The smile slipped and a blink freed the large droplets to slide down his face. "But there was nothing they could do for him. For either of them. And, yes, I wanted someone to pay for taking them away from me. But as angry as I was – and as desperate – I could never do what you're suggesting. It wouldn't be the people who tried to help us that I would go after, Detective."

"I quit the firm and came to work here." He looked around at his office, as if making sure in his mind he had made the right decision. "I get to help people every day, people with no place to go, addictions to overcome, demons to exorcise."

"People like you," Frankie ventured.

Wheeler looked up at him as if struck. Then he slowly nodded. "I never thought about it like that."

"You referred to little Ryan as 'our boy.' Even though you weren't his father, you still felt like he was yours, is that right?"

"Yes. I was going to adopt him once we were married."

"How did the boy's father – Randy Walken – feel about that?"

Wheeler scoffed. "Randy hasn't – hadn't even seen Ryan except once after he and Julia split up – for his first birthday."

"When did they split up?"

"When Ryan was three months old. I met Julia when he was eight months old. Randy never came to see her or his son other than the one time."

"Have you seen or spoken to him since the fire?"

Wheeler's jaw clenched and was slow to relax. "He had the decency not to come to the funerals. He sent some flowers to the funeral home, though. No card. He sent one to me, instead, saying that he was sorry for my loss. Said just because it hadn't worked out between them didn't mean he wasn't affected by what happened. But he admitted he had no business here and wouldn't be coming around, he just wanted me to know he was sorry and very saddened by it all." He sniffed and wiped his eyes. "It was the only decent thing the man ever did."

A very skinny woman with long unwashed hair entered the lobby outside Wheeler's office. Her eyes were red-rimmed and sunken, her pale skin scaly and taut. "Wheeler, I need to crash," she mumbled through the grille.

Joshua Wheeler stood and peered at her through the barrier. "Arms up, pockets out and do a little spin for me, Olivia."

The girl was already doing as he told. "I know the drill." She turned back toward him and put down her too thin arms. "Buzz me, I need to crash," she whined, chafing her palms against the front of her grimy jeans.

"Shoes, Liv. Then you go see Carla to drop her your clothes, then the shower, then some food."

"Yes, yes, yes," she muttered. "Okay, okay, but then I have to sleep."

"Yes. Then you can sleep."

The young woman kicked off her worn sneakers and upended them to show they were empty. Wheeler pushed a button on the wall and a loud buzzer indicated the lock on the inner door was released. Olivia pushed through, shoes in hand. "Thank you, Wheeler," she said in passing.

"Carla's in the next room back there," Wheeler informed her as she drifted away. "Excuse me, Detective," he said, grabbing a walkie-talkie. Frankie muttered a 'no problem' in reply, but Wheeler was already using the radio. "Carla- Olivia is on her way back to you now. Get her clothes searched and washed, make sure she showers and eats before she sleeps. She looks rough – make sure she's clean."

A woman's husky voice answered. "Got it. Cops if she's carrying?"

Wheeler smiled. "Got one right here. But she's too smart to bring junk in here. If she's using again, we'll just get her back in the program." He released the button on the radio and put it back on his desk.

"I can see you're busy," Frankie said. "If you think of anything that might be able to help us, I want you to call me," he handed him his card. "That's my desk at the station and that's my cell. All right?"

"All right. You really think someone from the apartments is doing this?"

"It's a lead we're pursuing," he replied by rote.

"Have you talked to a kid called Walt McMurty? He was a rough one, wild. His mother lived in the apartment next to ours – Cassandra McMurty. She died at the hospital that same night. Walt couldn't believe it when his sister told him he'd gotten there too late. He smashed his fist into a wall in the ER and walked out. His hand was no doubt broken, but he wouldn't let anyone touch it. I wouldn't have thought he was dangerous, but you never know, right?"

"I do have him on my list, but thank you." He stood and shook Wheeler's hand. Before he exited the office he turned back and asked, "By the way, how well did you know Bobby Avalon?"

"Bobby Avalon..." Wheeler said, thinking. "You mean the boxer?"

"That's right."

"Nobody knew him all that well. At least not those of us who were...how do I say this? Those of us who were on the level, let's just say. The guy lived almost like a rock star, people said. I guess it was 'cuz he was a bit of a celebrity in the area. There were some complaints from the people who lived closer to his apartment: people coming and going at all hours, people who looked like they were into some pretty heavy stuff. Most of us just made sure we weren't visible whenever they were around."

"Most, but not all?"

"Brookview wasn't exactly the Hilton, Detective. There were undesirables moving in and out all the time. It wasn't all that cheap to live there, either, though not as expensive as other, nicer places... A lot of them were people running drugs and the like, mostly."

"Did you ever see any of your neighbors associating with this crowd?"

"I never did personally, but I heard rumors the McMurty kid was trying to get in with them."

"Thank you, Mr. Wheeler. You've been extremely helpful," Frankie said with a parting nod.

Back in his car moments later, Frankie took out his list and crossed Joshua Wheeler's name off of it. As he drove away from the shelter, he dictated notes into a tape recorder. "Subject Joshua Wheeler, age thirty-one. Wears shoe size eleven, eyeball approximation, nearly the same size as me. Subject shows no overt signs of violent tendencies and was at work when the nurse was injured. Co-worker Carla Nunez confirmed alibi before showing me in to speak with Wheeler. He suggests Walt McMurty, age twenty-seven, as possible suspect. He's my next interview." Frankie stopped recording and made a left at the next intersection.

His phone rang. "Franks," he answered.

"Frankie, it's Conrad."

"Whatcha got, Ward?" He was stopped by a red light.

"We've pulled the hospital surveillance cameras. Tyler in A/V is going over it with a fine-toothed comb, but so far all we've got are some pretty poor visuals. The only person we couldn't positively ID is a white male, maybe twenty to thirty-five, wearing scrubs that were of a different pattern than what the hospital allows. No face, he keeps his head down. Tyler's trying to see if he can pull a reflection or something."

"Nice. Have him print me out a few stills, would you? No one I spoke to remembered anyone out of the ordinary, but maybe the visual will jog a few memories." He switched on his turn signal. "I'm gonna head over there now and take a look. It might help me narrow the suspect pool just on hair color and build alone."

"Exactly what I was thinking. I'll have them waiting for you."

"Thanks, Ward. See you in a few." He hung up and made the turn as the light changed, heading back to the crime lab. "You get a reprieve, Mr. McMurty. For now, anyway."

CHAPTER TWENTY

NOAH STOOD STARING into his steam-fogged bathroom mirror. Water dripped off the ends of his just cleaned dark hair into his eyes and traced trails over the jagged scars clawing across his cheekbone and temple. He closed his right eye, as he did several times every day, hoping to detect the slightest hint of light – anything at all. He was gazing in the direction he knew the light to be and...

He gave it thirty seconds. Then he gave it another thirty. A tear slid unbidden to mingle with the water on his face, its trail hot even against his shower-warmed skin. He opened his right eye and stared at the reflection of the glistening, salty droplet on his chin. A fierce anger welled up deep within him, erupting in an agonized growl and the thrusting of his fist through the mirror. With a crash, the mirror shattered, sending shards into the sink and onto the floor.

His growl of anger turned to a gasp of pain. Several slivers had sliced his hand and a few small pieces were embedded in his skin. Blood oozed down to his wrist and dripped into the sink. He grabbed up a towel and wrapped it around his hand, his movements rough and abrupt. Looking once more into the mirror, his reflection stared back at him in disjointed, shattered images. One shard held the teardrop, which clung still to his jaw.

He wiped it away.

A light but firm knock rapped on his door. Noah threw on an old grey 'Riverside University' tee-shirt and went to answer it. A glance through the peephole revealed his cousin Neil waiting in the hall. With a curious frown, Noah opened the door.

"Hey," Neil greeted him. "Got a minute?"

"Sure," Noah replied, stepping aside and gesturing him in with his towel-wrapped hand.

Neil's eyes went ever so slightly wide as he crossed the threshold and grabbed Noah's wrist. "What's this?"

Noah eyed him a second, attempting to quell his anger and embarrassment. "I broke the bathroom mirror."

Neil exhaled and looked his cousin over. When he noticed Noah's feet were bare beneath the hems of his jeans, he narrowed his eyes at him. "Surprised you didn't cut your feet, too." He unwrapped the towel and blinked. "You need this taken care of. Put on some shoes, I'll drive you to the ER."

Noah shrugged him off and rewrapped the towel. "I've got a kit, I'll take care of it." He headed toward the bathroom.

Neil brushed past him. "I got it. Go sit at the table," he ordered, stepping carefully onto the mirror-littered tile floor.

Noah seated himself at the small oak table in the alcove that served as a dining room and, after a few moments, Neil returned with a first-aid kit and a clean towel. He set these on the dining room table and retrieved a bowl from the kitchen, which he filled with scalding hot water before bringing it to the table. He didn't make a sound or change his expression, but Noah could feel the disapproval radiating off him.

From the kit he withdrew a pair of narrow-nosed forceps, steeped the ends in the hot water, and then swabbed them with a cotton ball soaked in alcohol. He spread the clean towel out and Noah laid his hand on it. Neil unwrapped the bloody towel and began to wipe away the blood with a gauze pad and alcohol. "What happened?"

Noah winced as the alcohol seeped into his wounds. "Some idiot shot a gun a quarter of an inch away from my face and after nine months I'm still half-blind and half-deaf." He kept his gaze fixed on his lacerated flesh. "You know they say when you lose one sense the others sort of compensate? Well, what's supposed to happen when you lose two senses, but only on one side?"

Neil removed a couple of slivers of glass, tweezing them out with the forceps. "I don't know. I guess you find another way to compensate. Or a way to deal." He rinsed the forceps in the water and went after another sliver.

"How the –" Noah started to retort, but thought better of it. "I'm being a jerk – did you need something? Is that why you came by?"

Neil flicked a glance at him. "Yeah, actually. I wanted to talk to you...about Monday."

"What's Monday?"

This time Neil looked completely away from his work. "My hearing. Nobody called you?"

"No," Noah returned, shocked. "Not the Turner case?"

"How often do you think I get accused of improper conduct? Yes, the Turner case. I was hoping you were going to testify."

"What about Frankie? Did they call him?"

"I don't know for sure but I assumed they had called both of you since you were the primaries on the case and were both there that day. If Frankie testifies, great. He knows my work, how I conduct my part of the investigation. But you know me. I could really use you in there."

"I'll make some calls to Special Services, try to talk to the Internal Affairs officer. I'll see what I can find out. I don't know if they'll let me make a statement, since they haven't contacted me about it, but I'll at least be there with you regardless. What time?"

"Nine o'clock. I know Cal and Ashton will be there, but I'm not sure what to expect from that. Sorry," he added in response to Noah's gasp of pain as he removed a sliver that was embedded especially deep.

"Did you do it?"

"Of course not."

"Did the lighter and the gas can have Turner's prints on them?"

"You know they did."

"Then you have nothing to worry about."

Neil removed the last bit of glass from Noah's hand, cleansed the wounds once more with the isopropyl alcohol and wound a length of gauze around his fingers down to his wrist. "You should still get this looked at. You may need a few stitches here and there." He tied off the bandage. "Are you okay? I mean, really?"

"I thought you came to ask me to help you, not so you could help me."

Neil quirked an eyebrow. "Do you need me to help you?"

"Don't start with the damned psychology bit. Your dad is the best shrink I know of and I've never let him get away with analyzing me – I'm sure as heck not going to let you do it."

"You put your hand through a mirror. I can tell just by looking at you and your place you haven't gone anywhere for a long time. What are you doing with yourself? What are you doing *to* yourself?"

Another flash of anger flared up inside. "What am I supposed to do, Neil? Compensate, find a way to deal? What can I do? I am maimed, a virtual cripple. I can't be a cop and I don't know how to be anything else. And what pisses me off most is the guy who did this to me is back on the street, and people keep expecting me to be okay and move on – but no one will tell me how!"

"Are you finished?"

"Yes!" Noah shouted, then, calmer, "Yes."

"Get your shoes on. You can shave on the way." Neil stood and began clearing the table.

Noah stared at him. "On the way to where?"

WITH THE BUZZ OF NOAH's electric razor providing discordant accompaniment to the quiet music playing over Neil's car speakers, they waded into the early afternoon traffic. Noah examined his shaven jaw in the visor mirror, listening to the song. He couldn't recall the name of the track, but he recognized the distinct voice of Ian McCulloch.

Neil flicked a glance at him. "As good as you're gonna get, I'm afraid," he observed dryly.

"Thanks," Noah replied in kind. "What are we doing?"

"Visiting a friend," came the vague reply.

After a few minutes of driving with Neil humming along, they passed a park where several children played, running and squealing behind the safety of a tall wrought-iron fence, and turned onto a tree-lined flagstone drive leading up to a stately brick building. They passed a brick signpost identifying the idyllic setting as the "Weymouth Estate."

"Wait," Noah tensed. "Where are we? This isn't your dad's-" he began, then frowned in confusion. "This isn't your dad's practice. What is this place?" Noah asked.

"You're right," Neil replied, pulling into the parking lot. "This isn't my dad's place." He parked near the entrance and shut off the car. "It's run by a friend of his, Doctor James Weymouth. He's a medical doctor, not a psychiatrist," he added to forestall Noah's imminent protests. "I talked to him about what happened to you. He'd heard about it on the news, was asking about your prognosis. He wanted you to come see him then, but I knew you wouldn't do it until you were ready." He appraised him with a critical eye. "I think you're ready now."

"Ready for what?"

Neil smiled and got out of the car. Noah remained seated, indecisive for a few seconds, watching the younger man's retreating back. Finally, curiosity won out and he followed his cousin into the building.

The interior had an atmosphere very much like a home: warm, inviting, safe. The walls were painted a warm shade of mocha and the plush carpet was a neutral shade similar to that of a pebble. The artwork adorning the walls looked to be the work of local artists, nothing fancy or expensive, just nice. Although there were overhead fluorescent lights, most were unused; amber-shaded floor lamps being opted for instead.

A pleasant, motherly sort of woman who sat behind a heavy cherry-wood desk broke into a huge smile upon looking up and seeing Neil. She stood and swept him up in a warm hug. "I wondered when we'd get to see you again! How are you?"

"Fantastic," Neil replied as deadpan as ever, but with a smile of his own.

Her gaze shifted to take in Noah, lingering on the scars for just a moment. She took one his hands into both of hers and said, "You must be Noah Harkham. The family resemblance is remarkable, almost like brothers. How are you, dear?"

Noah's unease seemed washed away by her radiant warmth. "A little at a loss for words, actually, Ms...?"

"Neil," she chided with a swat to his arm, "tell me you didn't bring him here without giving him the details." She rolled her sapphire eyes. "I'm Mrs. Weymouth, James' wife. Call me Betty." She linked her left arm with his right, keeping in his field of vision, and began steering him down a large hall. "Now, did Neil tell you anything before he kidnapped you?"

"Only that Doctor Weymouth had wanted me to come see him. Forgive me, Betty, but what is this place?"

"James runs the estate as a sort of rehabilitation facility for the visually- and/or hearing-impaired. We provide a safe environment in which people can learn to cope with their different abilities."

"Don't you mean disabilities?"

"Oh, no, Mr. Harkham," Betty returned, "not at all. Those whose vision or hearing has been taken away are given the ability to perceive the world in a whole new way. Our job is to help them learn how to use it." She showed them to a window opening into a glass-roofed sunroom. A small group of people ranging in age from six to about fifty sat in a semi-circle of comfortable padded chairs with desks attached, a tall, impressive man sitting in a similar chair before them. He was dressed in a simple, blue dress shirt and charcoal trousers; the sunlight streaming through the panes picked out bronze highlights in his short-cropped dark hair. He spoke animatedly, his authoritative yet friendly-sounding voice muffled by the glass.

"James is half-sided as well, Noah, on the right," Betty explained. "Fireworks accident when he was young. Lost his right eye completely. You'd never spot the prosthetic if you didn't know it was there, though, they've come such a long way these days. His hearing on that side is gone, as well."

"So he learned how to compensate for that side being useless?"

"Only the eye and ear are 'useless,' as you say. But he doesn't need to see or hear to know what's going on. He is every bit as aware - or maybe even more so - of what is happening around him as I or anyone else is. Most people have no idea James is any different than they are."

Noah caught Neil's slight smile as he watched him and Betty speaking. A spark of curiosity turned into cautiously-optimistic determination. He turned to Betty. "How?"

She patted his hand. "You shall see, my dear. You shall see."

CHAPTER TWENTY-ONE

———

"DETECTIVE HARKHAM," Dr. Weymouth said, welcoming Noah into his office with a friendly smile and handshake. The office was painted in soothing earthy colors, the furniture done in rich woods. Noah was surprised to see a fireplace in the wall to his right – complete with dancing flames – flanked by a couple of bookshelves. He almost felt like the good doctor should have greeted him decked out in a smoking jacket and pipe.

"Please, just Noah," he replied, taking a seat in the chair Dr. Weymouth indicated. "I'm not on the job anymore, as you can probably imagine."

Weymouth perched on the edge of his desk, steadying himself with one hand on its surface. "Noah," he conceded. "I was hoping to see you before now, but better late than never, isn't that what they say?" He favored his guest with a small smile that crinkled the corners of his eyes. Betty was right: he would never have guessed the right eye wasn't real. Even the particular shade of jade green in the iris was an exact match to the real one.

Noah cleared his throat. "To be honest, I didn't even know this place existed until today. Neil didn't think I was ready to come here before."

Weymouth tilted his head and peered at him. "Are you ready now?"

"I...think so. Betty says you're half-sided, too. How did you learn to function like everyone else again after it happened to you?"

"I didn't learn to function like everyone else. And neither will you."

Noah's heart went for a little plummet. "Oh. And so what would I learn?"

"How to function like someone with unilateral hearing and sight."
Again, he smiled, this time in a way that hinted at a world of secrets
hidden within those words.

Noah digested this for a minute. "But I can still have a normal life?
No more balance problems, depth-perception trip ups, having to
constantly check that I'm not talking too loud, that sort of thing?"

"In time you will overcome those problems and more – some you may
not be aware you are dealing with yet."

"How?" He was a little skeptical yet. "Why hasn't anyone talked about
this before?"

"I would wager a substantial amount of money none of your doctors
understand what it's like to be in our situation. I feel I can relate to
you on a whole different level than I can with even some of the other
patients I see here all the time. For instance, the ones who are totally
sightless or without hearing. I can help them because I can apply the
same methods to their situations with relative ease. But I don't
understand their plight nearly as well as I understand ours."

"Okay, I buy that. But that still doesn't tell me what it is you do. What
can you teach me?" He spread his hands. "How are you going to change
my life?"

Weymouth reached into his right pocket and pulled out a rubber ball,
which he started tossing up and catching with his right hand, all the
while keeping his eyes locked onto Noah. "Simple things, really. Like
how to trick your mind into not knowing it can't see or hear on one
side." He began to dance the ball across his knuckles and flip it from the
back of his hand over to his palm and back.

Noah chuckled. "I couldn't do that *before* I was injured."

"Well," Doctor Weymouth smiled, "we have two goals then. Let's get started. Catch." He threw the ball.

Noah reflexively reached for the ball as it streaked wide to his left side, and to his surprise, caught it. He looked from the ball clutched in his left hand to Dr. Weymouth, who watched him with a knowing glint in his eyes. A smile crept across Noah's face, crinkling the scars into new patterns.

"Not bad, for a start," the doctor commented. "Instinct and reflex are the building blocks, merely the foundation. Since it's been so long since you were injured, we're going to need to be aggressive in your training. It will be hard work and I won't go easy on you. Are you up for it?"

"Absolutely," Noah replied, tossing the ball back to his new coach.

———————

TWO HOURS LATER NEIL drove Noah back to his apartment, the former contentedly absorbed in another song and the latter replaying Weymouth's words in his mind. Neither said a word until they were back at the apartment, and then it was Noah who first broke the silence.

"It's all rubbish, you know that, right?"

Neil blinked, stopping in mid-stride. "Excuse me?"

"The Weymouth philosophy. 'There's no such thing as disabilities, only different abilities.' The loss or impairment of a sense is very much a disability. They just have to feed people that garbage to give them the placebo they need to heal."

"I thought you liked Doctor James," Neil said.

"I did. I do. But I don't buy the propaganda PC crap. His methods are sound, his treatment is excellent, but I think the philosophy is dangerous. By pretending I'm no different than anyone else, I put myself at risk of believing that it's true. At risk of forgetting there are certain things I can't do, or shouldn't do. But the way he's learned to use his other senses and his surroundings to supply him with the information his eye and ear can't – and the way he can teach other people to do it, too – is incredible." He gazed at his bandaged hand. "Thank you," he told Neil without looking up.

Neil put a hand on Noah's shoulder a moment, then walked to the door. Opening it, he said, "So, you're going back?"

"Yes."

"Same time? Two-thirty?"

"Sounds good."

"Want me to drive?"

A chuckle. "Yes, please."

"I'll pick you up tomorrow afternoon, then," he decided. "Take care, Noah," he added as he left.

CHAPTER TWENTY-TWO

———

WALT MCMURTY HADN'T been home, and when Frankie spoke with his employer, he was told Walt had the day off. Frankie moved on to the next names on the list, planning to come back to the kid later. Given the fuzzy picture Tyler had pulled from the surveillance camera, he had narrowed his suspect pool down to about half, leaving him with fourteen altogether. He had already spoken to eight of these potential suspects, and ruled them out, pending confirmation of alibis, so decided he'd earned a long, if late, lunch break.

He was still mulling over the information Parker and Conrad had given him about the coffeemaker... For the blast to be so small and contained, it did seem to indicate this guy wasn't looking to kill. However, shooting someone in the gut was usually a sign you wanted them dead - and be in agony along the way. So now he wasn't sure what he was dealing with, but he'd rather assume this guy meant business and try to be prepared for the worst.

All the uniformed cops and detectives had been advised to wear body armor for the time being. All these precautions were great, but they were still no closer to finding this guy. And until they did...

He took a seat at his favorite diner - called the Surfside Café, although the closest beach was actually five miles away in the next town. His usual waitress, Jean, sidled up to his table and smiled. "What can I get you today, Frankie?"

"The special, please," he said, giving her a smile of his own. "And a large Coke."

"You got it. Steak and loaded baked potato and a large Coke coming right up. You staying or do you want it bagged up to go?"

"Nah, I'm staying today. Treating myself to a long lunch."

Her eyes lit up and she leaned in conspiratorially, although her voice stayed the same volume. "So does this mean you and your boys are close to catchin' this guy? You know, the one who shot the fireman and hurt that nurse."

"You know I can't discuss an active investigation with you," he replied in mock sternness. "Besides, what makes you think it's the same guy?"

She snorted. "Please, honey – I may be a waitress but I'm not stupid. Two attacks in just a few days, both on emergency service types – and both with your name attached to the case? That practically screams 'serial' to me. And the way they were attacked!" She laid a hand on her ample chest. "Granted the gun wasn't very original, but getting in and setting the fire without setting off an alarm or getting on camera, now that's smart. And rigging up a coffee maker to burn up whenever someone touched it was pretty damn ingenious. Terrifying, yes – but clever. It's like he's some sort of MacGyver or something."

Frankie noticed several other diners were now trying very hard not to look like they were listening, as Jean hadn't bothered to keep her voice quiet. A couple of thoughts occurred to him simultaneously as her words struck a chord with him. "Actually, Jean, make my order to go," he said, getting up.

She scribbled something on her order pad with a slight sigh. He smiled at her. "Just keep watching the news. You'll know what we know as soon as we can release it."

"Whatever you say, honey. I'll have your food out in just a bit." She went back to the kitchen to place the order.

Frankie met her at the register and settled his bill. While he waited for his order, he mulled over the thoughts that had occurred to him while they had been talking. He figured the best thing to do would be to check the phone book and get a map. When she returned with his food, he asked, "Jean, do you have a phone book I could borrow?"

"Sure thing, honey," she said, reaching under the counter. She handed him a somewhat greasy Calera County phone book.

"Thanks, you're a life saver," he told her with a wink.

As he headed toward the door, she called after him, "Hey, what are you-?"

"I'll bring it back, Jean, promise." He crossed his heart with one finger. She waved him off with a dish towel and a resigned smile.

Once he got back into his car, he opened the phone book to the listings for hardware stores and discount department stores - locations where a "MacGyver" could get whatever he needed to plan his attacks. Then he retrieved the city map he kept in his glove compartment. There were five hardware stores and four department stores within a radius of thirty blocks from both the hospital and the fire station. He circled their locations on the map.

He then perused his suspect list, noting the locations of each one's residence and place of work. He then drew a circle encompassing the rough thirty-block radius and made a new list of only those names that fell within the overlapping areas, since most killers operated inside their own neighborhood. Interestingly enough, he noticed, the Brookview apartment building also lay well within the overlap, as did one particularly eye-catching name: Walt McMurty.

He swore under his breath. He grabbed his radio and alerted Dispatch to put out a BOLO on McMurty, forwarding a description of the vehicle registered in his name, so all available units could lend their eyes to the search. He drove by McMurty's house again, but he still wasn't there. He drummed his fingers on the steering wheel indecisively for a moment.

Finally he flipped open his cell phone and called Ziehring, asking for a uniformed unit to be sent to the house for surveillance. He wanted to pursue the store camera lead, he explained. Ziehring agreed and Frankie waited less than fifteen minutes for a pair of officers in an unmarked car to arrive. He briefed them before speeding off to the nearest store on the list.

The store clerk confirmed McMurty often came into the store and had been there the day the firefighter was attacked, but said the man in the hospital surveillance still did not, indeed, look like Walt. Although, he added, Walt does have dark hair like the man in the photo, and, yes, he is about the same height...

Frankie pressed the clerk to play the tape for the day of the shooting and sure enough, Walt had come into the store that day. However, he was able to tell that he had not purchased any wire strippers or screwdrivers. He had bought a couple of paint brushes, paint tray and blue painter's tape instead. He could have given himself the five finger discount, Frankie suggested, but the clerk denied the possibility. But he agreed to hand over the surveillance tapes for the last week.

"Maybe you're right, maybe not," he said amiably to the older man, "but either way, I hafta take these tapes with me for a while. You'll get them back once we're done with them, you have my word."

"The word of a police officer meant something, time was. But these days," he waved his hand and made a negative sound. "All right, go on and take it. But Walt is a good young man – not some monster. You'll see."

"Do you have any idea where he might be right now?"

"He comes in, he buys light bulbs or things to make his old house look nicer, we talk about the weather and local whatnot, he leaves. That's all I know. He's very polite, nice to an old man like me because he says I remind him of his grandfather. I don't know nothing about where he likes to go or what he likes to do. But I know he is no killer." He held out the tape and jutted out his jaw.

"I hope for his sake you're right," Frankie said, taking the tapes and leaving. He then collected the security tapes from the other eight stores for the days of the attacks, just in case it turned out McMurty wasn't their guy or if he'd shopped somewhere else. The circumstantial evidence was beginning to look good; however, their A/V guy would have to run some more comparisons against the man in the hospital tape to be sure.

———————

IT WAS EVENING BY THE time Frankie got the tapes over to the lab. Ward met him outside the door of the Audio/Visual Lab, having just come to check up on Tyler's progress on recovering a reflection.

"How long have you been here, Ward?" Frankie asked, remembering Conrad usually worked second shift, but had called him early this morning.

"Since about nine this morning," he replied, holding the door for the detective.

"And you're on tonight, too?"

"Mmm-hmm. Only until midnight. I had a couple hours' break in between, though. Neil's out until after the hearing, so I put in for some overtime hours to catch up on my share of his workload. I've been fiendin' to get back to my ocean and surf for, like, a week straight, so I need the extra cash. As much as we need Neil back, this is actually doing me a favor, I hate to say."

He opened the A/V lab door. "Hey there, Seoul brother," he said to Tyler Hendricks, the A/V tech. "Special delivery," he indicated the box of tapes Frankie carried in.

Tyler threw him a fed-up glare. "Half-Seoul brother," Conrad corrected.

"Dude, my mother is from Iksan. She's never even been to Seoul." He spun his ergonomic computer chair toward them and squared his broad shoulders. "What've we got now, Detective?" He eyed the box warily.

"These are security camera tapes from the nine locations our suspect is most likely to have bought that wire stripper. Since you guys didn't find any trace evidence on the package from anywhere other than the hospital lounge, I figured it was probably new, bought on the way. I want us to have a look and see if we can find someone who matches the suspect on the hospital tape."

"Oh, yeah," Conrad said, snapping his fingers, "I forgot to tell you this morning: we pulled a price off the tag. It was for eight dollars and some – the rest was missing. No store name or logo on the bit we recovered, though, just a generic white sticker."

Frankie nodded, thinking. "That's pretty standard for the smaller Mom-and-Pop type places. All of the locations sold wire strippers and pliers in the week before the attacks, but I didn't think to ask them how much they sold for. I'll make some calls, narrow down the focus some more."

"I'll do it, Frankie," Conrad offered. "I thought I mentioned it earlier, but I guess I forgot. I'll take care of it."

Frankie looked at his watch: 6:48. "Yeah, okay. I did manage to find out one suspect had been in one of these stores the day of the shooting, I'll stick around and see if we can get a good comparison to the hospital surveillance footage." He handed Conrad the yellow page listings. "I circled the ones I have tapes for. Thanks."

"No problem. Oh, Tyler, any luck grabbing a reflection?"

"Nothing that will be of much use, I'm afraid. The glass in the break-room's door caught a partial reflection, but it's a small area. I'm not sure it will give many identifying features, but I'm trying to clean it up some more. This guy looks like he was aware of the cameras and took every step to avoid being picked up on them. He knew what he was doing."

"Work some magic for us, Ty," Ward said with a wink as he exited the room.

Frankie gave Tyler the tape from the hardware store McMurty had been to the day of the shooting. It took him a few minutes to isolate and copy the image of McMurty and use a program to lay it side by side with the image from the hospital footage. The images were from opposite angles, so he rotated the hardware store image to the same angle as the other.

"That didn't help too much," Conrad observed as he came back in the room a few minutes later. "Seven of the stores sell some type of wire strippers for the eight dollar price range, but only five of them use the generic white stickers. So all I was able to do was eliminate the Shop and Save, Bill's Hardware, Ames Hardware, and the Lo-Mart."

"That still keeps McMurty in the running," he replied. "He was at Laughlin's Hardware." He pointed to the screen.

Conrad took a look. "Similar hair, similar build. Who did you say this is?"

"Walt McMurty. He lives less than five blocks away from both the fire station and Laughlin's Hardware, which is about another ten blocks from the hospital. He works at an auto repair shop, also less than five blocks from the fire station, and was off the clock at the time of both assaults."

"Why isn't he in custody for questioning already?"

"Because no one can find him."

"Here we go," Tyler cut in. "I reversed and rotated the image from the hardware store to match it up with the one from the hospital. Side by side and overlay comparisons..." he clicked on an icon on the screen and the images flickered beneath a little hour glass, then stopped. "Looks like seventy-five percent chance it's the same guy," he said, reading the results from a small window that had popped up.

"Seventy-five? That's it?" Frankie was surprised and a little disappointed.

"That's the best I can say with these two clips. The program is pretty accurate, though."

"Okay, let's review the other tapes and see if we can grab anyone else who buys wire strippers."

"I don't know if you noticed, but McMurty didn't buy one," Tyler pointed out.

"Yeah, you're right..." Frankie pulled on his lower lip while he thought it over. "He could have lifted it, though. Shoved it inside his jacket."

"Ah, well, for that you'll have to give me an hour or so. I can compare the geometric appearance of the jacket – angles, shadows, dimensions and so on – before and after he goes up to the register. If he put something in his jacket after he walked through the front door it will alter the structure, the contours of the material. Sometimes it's pronounced enough to reconstruct the exact shape of the item. But, like I said, it takes some time."

"Do it," Frankie ordered. "I'll get started on the other tapes over here."

CHAPTER TWENTY-THREE

FRANKIE STUCK AROUND to help view the tapes for another hour, then realized if he was going to act on the second idea that had occurred to him at the diner, he'd be better off starting tonight. He took his leave of Tyler and Conrad, and drove back to the precinct. He found Ziehring still in his office, as he expected, and knocked on his captain's door.

"Come in."

Frankie entered and Ziehring looked up from a stack of paperwork in his hand. "What can I do for you, Franks?"

"I think we should have another press conference."

Ziehring set the paperwork aside. "Have a seat," he gestured to an empty chair across from his desk, his brow furrowed. "What have you got in mind?" Ziehring smoothed his gray tie.

"I was thinking earlier today how smart this guy is. If we play that up in the media, appeal to his arrogance, I'm thinking he may try to contact us. Especially if we temper it with a few disparaging comments on his lack of success. We'll call him a failed serial killer. That should get some sort of response."

"I'm afraid it would." The captain thought it over, scratching at the nape of his red hair. "This sounds a little too risky to me. What if all it does is trigger another attack?"

"That's why I want to be the one to talk to the media. I want him to see my face, know my name."

"You want to be bait."

"Yes, sir."

"I can't let you do that." Ziehring fixed him with a level stare, his green eyes boring into Frankie's. "I'm not in the habit of throwing my men to the wolves."

"Sir, I think this will work. I think I can lure him out. Besides," he said, trying to sound nonchalant, "I think I may already be in his sights."

Ziehring leaned back. "What are you talking about?"

"You know I've been running on the theory that this guy is targeting rescue personnel. Well, now I think it's specifically rescue personnel involved in a fire-related death. I've been looking into the Brookview fire, since it was the most recent one. Now, so far he's tried to kill –or at least has attacked – a firefighter from the fire station that responded to the call and a nurse from the hospital all the victims were taken to. The next step is to go after the cops who investigated it. That would be me, specifically, and a handful of uniformed officers who provided support."

"Weren't you the one who said he hadn't been targeting specific people – that the attacks were random?"

"They have been. I want to change that. I want him to come after me, give him a specific target. That way, he'll be easier to catch."

"Unless he's too smart to fall for it," Ziehring countered.

"Then the whole force stays on high alert."

"And the Brookview connection? How do you plan to play that out?"

"I've been debating that, sir. What do you think?"

Ziehring considered the matter for a moment. "I think we should keep it under wraps for now. That should help weed out false leads."

Frankie nodded. "All right. So I've got the green light?"

"This could be a very bad idea, you know," Ziehring sighed. "Or even a waste of time."

"But there's only one way to find out for sure."

Frankie watched as his captain wrestled with the decision. "All right," he finally said. "Do it. But I hope for your sake you know what you're getting yourself into."

"I do."

"Now, let's go over what you're going to say. I want this scripted down to a science. Hopefully we can still get it aired on the ten o'clock news tonight, or at least tomorrow morning." Ziehring sighed. "This had better work, Detective."

CHAPTER TWENTY-FOUR

———

NOAH WAS STILL GETTING ready when Neil arrived at his apartment Friday afternoon. He let his cousin in and told him to make himself at home while he finished up. Noah had changed into workout pants and an old police department tee shirt for today's session, since Dr. James had told him to expect some physical training. He was in the bathroom applying a special scar cream to the left side of his face when he heard a knock on his door.

"Got it," Neil called to him. There was a second of silence as Neil presumably looked through the peephole. "Uh, your pizza's here," Neil announced with a question in his voice.

Noah frowned. "I didn't order - Neil, wait!" He charged into the living room just as the 'delivery guy' shoved his black jacket-clad arm through the partially opened door to plunge something shiny into the side of Neil's neck.

Horrified, he watched as Neil grabbed the man's wrist and shoved the door closed on his arm in an effort to make him release his grip on the weapon. Noah was already running toward his cousin, fear making his movements feel far too slow. He drew Neil's nine-millimeter from his hip holster and the shot the attacker in the upper arm.

The assailant let go of the weapon and jerked his arm back through the door with a short scream. Noah caught Neil as his legs gave way beneath him and lowered him to the floor. He ducked out into the hall and dialed 911. There was no sign of the man now, but he did see a trail of blood on the floor and knew it would only be a matter of checking with hospitals to find this guy.

The 911 operator answered. "I need an ambulance at 79 Slate Street, apartment 3-A. The victim is Neil Coates, a criminalist with the county crime lab." He ducked back into the apartment.

"Okay, sir, what is your name?"

"Noah Harkham, retired Detective Sergeant, Riverdale PD. I need that bus here ASAP."

He knelt next to Neil, laying the phone, on speaker, on the floor next to him. Neil's right hand was clamped around the object imbedded in the base of his neck, which Noah now realized was a large piece of mirrored glass. A streak of scarlet gushed out of the corner of Neil's mouth as he struggled to speak. Noah's insides clenched and his blood ran cold, driving all other thought but to save Neil from his mind.

"Don't talk," he said, his voice thick in his dry mouth. He squeezed Neil's left hand in his, and wrapped his other hand over Neil's right to help stabilize the glass. "Help's coming, Neil, just hang on."

"S-sorry," Neil whispered.

"No, don't say that, it wasn't-" Noah started, but Neil grunted a weak protest.

"No...He said..."

"He said he was sorry? The assailant?"

Neil blinked slowly and half-whispered, "Yes."

"Okay, stay still, all right? Don't move, don't try to talk. We're going to get you taken care of. Just as soon as they get here," he added under his breath with a worried glance at the phone. "Where the hell is that ambulance? The hospital is less than a mile from here!"

"Sir, stay calm. They are on the way right now. I need more information. Is the victim still conscious?"

"Yes."

"Okay. What happened? How is he injured?"

"There's a large shard of glass imbedded in the side of his throat, the right side. I don't know how deep it is."

"The officer was stabbed in the throat with a piece of glass?"

"Yes. We have it manually immobilized. I shot the attacker with the victim's gun – I need you to notify Detective Alan Franks with the Fifth Precinct to run a check at all area hospitals for a white male, approximately five foot six, wearing a dark jacket with a GSW to the upper left arm. Tell him I said that's our guy. Do you copy?"

"Yes, sir, Detective. I've got someone notifying him as we speak." A slight pause. "The ambulance is at the building right now. They're on the way up to your apartment."

"Thank you," he said, turning his attention back to Neil. The younger man's eyes were beginning to roll and he gurgled up more blood, spilling it out down his chin.

"Hey, hey, now, none of that," he said, squeezing Neil's left hand. Neil's eyes focused on Noah again. "That's it. Look at me."

He was shaking, his voice trembling. He had to stay calm and keep Neil focused. Neil's eyelids were getting heavy and Noah felt his hand going slack under his. "Hey, you gotta stay awake, okay?"

The sound of the paramedics' footfalls on the stairs was an almost tangible relief. "They're here, Neil. You're going to be okay. You hear me?"

Neil was barely conscious, but he did whisper, "Okay."

"In here!" Noah called out as the sound of the paramedics got closer. A moment later, they rushed in and carefully removed both Noah's and Neil's hands from the glass, immobilizing it with rolls of gauze packed on either side.

Noah sat back on his heels watching them work. "He's allergic to latex," he remembered.

Got it," one of the medics, a middle-aged Latino whose nameplate identified as *S. Esposito*, said. "I'll make sure the hospital knows," he told his partner, a younger petite blonde. *N. Davis*, her nameplate said.

"Right," she replied. "Starting an IV. Sir, can you hear me? What's his name?" She flashed brilliant blue eyes at Noah.

"Neil."

"All right, Neil, I'm inserting a needle into your left arm now, okay?" She did the procedure in less than a few seconds. She cradled the bag of fluids between her shoulder and chin. "How's he looking?"

Her partner was checking Neil's vitals. He gave her a grim look that made Noah's heart stutter. "We need to move him now."

She helped him get Neil onto a backboard and the two of them hoisted him up on the gurney. As they pushed the gurney into the hall, the blonde gave Noah a reassuring smile. "Good job keeping the glass immobile. You may have just saved his life."

Noah just nodded. Once they were out of the apartment, he took a moment to double over and run a shaky hand over his face. He stared at the bloodstain on the carpet as he picked up his phone. Then he followed the medics out to the ambulance.

They allowed him to climb into the ambulance with Neil, but made sure he kept out of the way. The older paramedic climbed in behind the wheel and the ambulance rocketed out of the parking lot, siren blaring. The girl worked with practiced hands to secure Neil's airway and maintain his blood pressure, the whole time spouting off an array of terms and stats to the driver that Noah didn't understand.

Noah watched it all, terrified, as the ambulance sped them toward the hospital.

CHAPTER TWENTY-FIVE

———

"There may be times when we are powerless to prevent injustice, but there must never be a time when we fail to protest."

- Elie Wiesel

PAIN UNLIKE ANY HE'd ever felt - like fire and ice battling for dominion - lanced through his arm from his shattered shoulder down to his cold, half-numb fingertips. His mind raced – he knew he had to get to a hospital or he'd bleed to death, but he was sure the cops would be looking for him there. He had to do something fast. Sirens wailed somewhere down the street, rapidly getting closer: an ambulance.

He wasn't sure what had happened, what had gone wrong. The former detective lived alone, he had found out; there shouldn't have been anyone there to help him. But someone else had been there, someone who had had the quick wits to use the detective's gun to shoot him. It hadn't happened the way he wanted, no, not at all. Just like with the firefighter...

If they hadn't failed to understand his message twice now, he wouldn't have had to come after the former cop at all. He had heard the detective in the diner – the one whose face was on every TV he saw – and knew he still had work to do. He didn't want to have to kill anyone, but he had run out of options. So many had died in the tragedy, so much terrible damage had been inflicted before they were even aware of the one who was responsible. They'd gotten him, in the end, but far too late.

All because they had ignored *his* warning.

And now there was a chance the killer could go free, and the crime would go unpunished. It was a thought too terrible to contemplate. But to kill a cop...

But to kill a former cop, one who was so obviously living in misery, well, that was almost a service. He could put an end to the man's purposeless half-life and, maybe, get the closure they all needed, the justice the victims deserved - if only they would put it all together, finally understand.

He had to live long enough to make sure they did.

CHAPTER TWENTY-SIX

———

CONRAD WAS GETTING cross-eyed, and he'd only been staring at the monitor for an hour so far. He and Tyler had met up in the A/V lab around nine o'clock to dig in on the footage they hadn't gotten to last night. He sighed and glanced over to see if Tyler was having as much fun as he was.

Tyler rubbed his eyes and took another sip of his coffee. "Remind me not to let you make the coffee next time," he said.

"What's wrong with it?" Conrad demanded.

"Oh, nothing, if you like fairy piss," he replied sweetly.

"Too weak?"

"Yeah, and what's with that... fruity, herbal aftertaste?"

"Red tea. It's good for the immune system and helps prevent ulcers."

"Dude, that is so Californian," Tyler commented in his best surfer voice.

"That's why I didn't tell you what it was before you drank it: knew you wouldn't have an open mind." Well, that and it was just fun to see people's faces when they take the first sip. "And for the record, I don't sound like that."

"Whatever, you totally do. And forgive me for not subscribing to weird," Tyler retorted. He stretched and yawned. "Even in fast forward this is taking forever."

"Yeah, riveting, huh? And notice how Frankie had more important things to do today."

"What's Lewis and Saddler doing? Aren't they getting in on this action?"

"Nah, they're still working that subway train thing across town – the engineer was found dead in the control car. Someone decided to check on him after he failed to stop at three consecutive stations. The ME ruled it homicide; there was a small hole in the base of his skull."

"And a whole train full of suspects to process," Tyler commiserated. "Finally," he breathed. "Got another one."

Conrad paused the tape he was viewing and stepped over to Tyler's screen. "I don't recognize him," he frowned. "Let's get a good face shot and I'll run it against the mugshots, like the others."

An urgent tapping on the A/V room door preceded the entrance of Cal Parker, his skin ashen and his expression one of suppressed grimness. "Conrad, get your kit. We have to go."

Conrad's blood went cold with inexplicable fear. "What is it?" he asked, rising to stand.

"He's attacked again." His control over his expression faltered. "It's Neil."

Conrad steadied himself on the back of Tyler's chair. "God, no," Tyler murmured.

Conrad swallowed past the constriction in his throat. "Let's go," he said, striding past Parker.

———————

"TELL ME," CONRAD DEMANDED as he and Parker walked to collect his kit.

"He's alive – so far. Single stab wound to the throat. He was taken to County."

"County? But he lives closer to Memorial."

"He was attacked at Noah's apartment. Franks believes Harkham was the intended target." They picked up Conrad's kit and rushed to the parking garage. "Frankie and Noah are at the hospital now. I want you there, too – get the weapon, his clothes, nail scrapings and photos as soon as possible. I'm going to the apartment; I'll meet you at the hospital when I'm through."

They arrived at Parker's SUV. "Noah was able to injure the attacker – GSW to the upper arm. Frankie's got his guys checking every clinic, hospital and doctor's office in the area. It's only a matter of time, but we have to have the evidence in place to compare to him." He got into his vehicle and fixed Conrad with a piercing gaze. "We have to catch him this time."

Conrad nodded, determined. "Cal," he said, his voice wavering, "he's not going to make it, is he?"

"I don't know, Con. I really don't know."

CHAPTER TWENTY-SEVEN

———

CONRAD NARROWLY AVOIDED colliding with a nurse as he pushed his way past a knot of ER staff rushing a screaming woman on a gurney down the crowded hallway. He approached the check-in desk and showed the clerk his identification. "I'm Conrad Ward with the county crime lab. There was a stab wound victim brought in about half an hour ago – Neil Coates. Where can I find him?" His hands were trembling.

The clerk checked the computer. "Ummm...yeah, they just took him up to surgery," the young man replied, idly rubbing his stubbled jaw with the fingertips of one hand.

"He's alive," Conrad breathed out a grateful sigh. "What about the detectives who came with him? Detective Franks and Noah Harkham, where can I find them?"

"They went to the surgical ward waiting room. Second floor."

"Thanks," he said. "I'm also going to need his clothes and the weapon."

"The cops should be holding those for you. The ER doctors bagged it all."

He nodded. "Second floor?" The clerk confirmed this with a nod and Conrad hurried toward the stairs. He located the waiting room and there he found Frankie and Noah – the former talking on a pay phone in the hall just outside the door, the latter sitting on a couch, staring at his shaking hands.

Conrad nodded a grim greeting to Frankie then strode into the room. "Hark," he said as he entered.

Noah looked up as if dazed and stood. Recognition then seemed to register on his face and he took a step forward. "Ward – thank God." His voice was tired and strained.

Conrad approached and laid a hand on the former detective's shoulder, steering him back to the couch. "Harkham – what happened up there today?"

Again, Noah looked down at his hands, but this time he seemed to notice they were trembling; he clenched them into tight fists and pressed them against his thighs. Conrad nodded to the bandage on his right hand and asked, "Did he hurt you, too?"

He shook his head. "No, I did this all on my own." He stared at the floor. "It's my fault," he continued, his voice flat and leaden. "He was at the door – dressed like a pizza guy – and Neil didn't realize. He opened the door and the guy just...I came in but he'd already stabbed him and I couldn't..." he shook his head slowly. "I couldn't stop it. I shot him, in the arm, though." He ran a hand over his face and then rubbed the back of his neck. "At least I did that much right," he muttered.

"Quick thinking. I didn't know you had a gun anymore," Conrad said, and regretted it the moment it came out of his mouth. He knew from Neil that Noah had had to give his gun to Frankie not too long after he was forced to retire, after nearly turning it on himself.

"I used Neil's."

"Neil was wearing his gun? That's weird."

"It's his," Noah shrugged. "He's got the permit and every right to have it on him if he wants."

"Yeah, but, I mean – he's on 'vacation' pending the hearing..." But then, he remembered Neil had told him once in passing that he felt vulnerable without a weapon because of something that had happened to him a long time ago and so had gotten a lifelong permit to carry. Conrad had never found out what this something was, but he was now grateful it had happened. It had potentially saved Neil's life today.

Frankie came in, followed by Officer Branson and both men shook hands with Conrad. Frankie handed him a few paper bags, explaining each in turn. "His shirt, his pants, his shoes and this," he handed over a metal tray with a large shard of bloodied glass lying inside, "is the weapon. I've made some calls, but so far the attacker hasn't turned up in any of the usual places."

"More than likely this guy knows someone under the radar to go to for this sort of thing. I'm sure he's smart enough to realize the whole department is looking for him," Conrad replied.

"We're looking into that, too," Branson assured him. "Cox and Adelmo and a bunch of the others are checking leads."

"How long until we know anything about Neil?" Conrad asked.

Frankie shrugged, shooting Noah a sympathetic look. "I don't know, but given the injury, I'd say the longer it takes the better chances of it being good news, you know?"

"Yeah, I guess so," Conrad agreed. "Did you call his family yet?"

"Yeah. I called his dad when I got here, they were out of town but should be here soon. How are the security tapes coming?"

"Tyler pulled some more images and ran that program on McMurty's jacket."

"And?"

"So far, nothing. He's clean. And we haven't found anyone in the tapes yet that is an exact match." He shook his head in frustration. "We've got nothing so far."

Noah, who had all this time been sitting on the couch and staring at the waiting room doorway, now turned his attention to them. "Where's Parker?"

Conrad turned to him, somewhat surprised by the abrupt question. "He's at your apartment, processing. Why?"

"The glass – it's mirrored, isn't it?"

Frankie gave him a look. "Yeah. I think it looked like it was. I didn't touch it, though," he added to Conrad.

Noah groaned, but he seemed to have snapped out of his shocked daze. "I think it came from my bathroom mirror."

Conrad frowned. "What are you talking about?"

Noah held up his bandaged hand. "Yesterday, I put my hand through the mirror. Neil came by just after; he bandaged me up. We left for a while, but when I got back I cleaned up all the glass and put it in the trash can."

"And threw it in the Dumpster outside," Branson supposed.

Noah gave him a significant look. "No. It was late. I just tied off the bag and left it in the bathroom. I was going to toss it out on our way out today." He paused. "Somehow, he got into my apartment while I was gone, took a piece of the mirror, and came back today to kill me with it."

"I'll call Cal," Conrad said, turning toward the door.

"I should have taken precautions. First the firefighter, then the nurse. Fire-related deaths, I said. It's Brookview, isn't it? Of course he was going to come after one of us. That's what you were thinking that night, right?"

"Brookview?" Branson asked.

"Wait," Conrad said from where he'd stopped in midstride on his way out the door, "you knew this might happen? You knew and you did nothing? Why didn't you tell us? Why didn't you tell him?" Conrad made an angry gesture toward the surgical ward. "He worked that case, too – why the hell didn't either of you say something?"

"I thought he'd come after us, cops," Frankie said. "I never felt you all were at risk. Other than Neil getting the arson kit from Turner, the lab was barely involved at the scene. Noah did most of the processing himself – and I thought he'd be safe since he's not on the force anymore. This guy has been attacking random people, no one specific yet, so I alerted the force to a possible threat, got everyone in body armor. I did the press conferences, made sure he would see my face. I thought if he went after anyone specific this time it would be me. It was supposed to be me." He hugged his arms around his middle, his eyes brimming with unshed tears.

"I'm sure that will be a real comfort to his parents if they have to put him in the ground," Conrad said, piercing the guilt-ridden detective with a dark look. His glare shifted briefly to Noah, then he stalked out of the room, evidence in hand.

HE NEEDED FRESH AIR and distance, so he went all the way downstairs to his SUV and logged all the evidence, storing it in the climate controlled lock box, before calling Parker. He dialed the number and took a deep breath, letting it out noisily to calm himself. His boss answered after half a ring.

"Parker."

"It's Ward. Neil's still alive, as far as I know. He's in surgery, but they aren't telling us anything more than that."

"Okay," he said, sounding relieved. "Keep me posted."

"Of course. Listen, Cal – Hark says the glass the guy used might have come from the apartment. There's a trash can –"

"In the bathroom. Yes, I'm looking at it right now. There were signs the attacker picked the locks, so I knew he'd been here before the attack. The bathroom mirror caught my eye."

Conrad answered his unspoken question. "Apparently, Noah and the mirror had a little misunderstanding. He says he was gone for a while and cleaned up the mess when he got back."

"Don't worry, if there's anything to be found, I'll find it. He left plenty of his DNA behind this time, thanks to Harkham. Judging from the amount of blood in the trail from the apartment, if he doesn't show up for medical care soon, he'll show up as our next suspicious death."

"Frankie has Cox and Adelmo and some others heading the search right now. It shouldn't take long. I'll let you know as soon as they tell us anything."

"Right. And if I'm not there when he comes out of surgery, let me know what the doctors say. This scene is pretty straightforward, though, so it shouldn't take me too much longer. I'll follow the blood trail as far as I can, maybe I'll get lucky."

"Great. See you when you get here then."

"Yep," Parker said, hanging up.

Ward pocketed his phone and started back inside. Just as he got to the door he heard someone call his name. He turned to see Shots hurrying across the lot. "Ward," she said as she caught up with him. "I tried to call you – is it true? Neil was attacked?"

Her eyes were wide and she was shaking. "He was. He's in surgery, but I don't know anything else yet."

She put a hand to the silver cross on her necklace. "What are his chances?"

He took a deep breath before answering. "He's strong, healthy–"

"Conrad," she pleaded, putting a hand on his arm. He was surprised to see how worried she was. Robin had only transferred in from a smaller lab less than a year ago when the previous ballistics tech, O'Brien, had retired. And although all the criminalists liked and respected her, he hadn't realized she and Neil were that close.

He looked her in the eye. "Not good, maybe. I don't know," he admitted, a slight quiver in his voice that he tried to disguise by clearing his throat. His beeper went off, interrupting the tense moment. He frowned. It was Captain Ziehring.

"Excuse me," he said, calling the captain back. "This is Ward. What's up?"

"I just got a call from the hospital. Amy Simpson, the nurse, died almost an hour ago. Franks has his phone turned off and Parker said you were there with him. Let him know this just became a homicide investigation, all right?"

"Yes, sir," he sighed. "I will. But I don't understand, the fire didn't cause any injuries, right? I thought it was just a mild panic attack or something."

"I don't know the details, but it seems she had a pre-existing heart condition and just couldn't recover from the heart attack. What's the word on Coates?"

"Nothing yet. He's still in surgery."

"Okay. Thanks, Ward."

"You bet," Conrad replied as Ziehring disconnected the call. He hung up and was silent a long moment, his fingers laced at the back of his neck. His thoughts were jumbled, but one lingered in the forefront of his mind, one that made him feel sick. "Oh, man," he said, dropping his hands.

Robin touched his arm lightly. "What's wrong?"

"That was Ziehring. The nurse died about an hour ago."

"Oh, no."

"Yeah. But you know what my first thought was? If only she had died a few hours sooner, maybe this guy wouldn't have come after Noah – maybe Neil wouldn't have been attacked. Nice, huh?" He nodded toward the necklace she still held. "Wonder what kind of person He'd say that makes me."

"One who's only human. You're just worried about a friend. And you didn't really mean it. If you had, you wouldn't feel so guilty."

He regarded her a moment. "Come on, we should go up in case there's any news."

CHAPTER TWENTY-EIGHT

———

WHEN SHE AND CONRAD arrived back at the waiting room, Robin noticed Noah wasn't there with the others. Frankie was seated on one of the small couches. Officer Branson was staring out the window. Robin could feel tension infuse the room as soon as Conrad entered it, especially between him and Frankie, and though curious to the origin of it, she didn't ask. She tried to fade into the background.

"Ziehring called," Conrad told Frankie tersely. "He got a call from Memorial. The nurse is dead. Thought you should know we're dealing with a homicide now."

"What?" Noah asked, stopped in his tracks in the doorway, all the color drained from his face. "What did you just say?"

"No, not Neil," Conrad started to explain.

Frankie jumped up and interrupted him. "It's the nurse, Hark. We haven't heard anything about Neil yet."

Noah sagged against the door frame. "Oh, thank God." He shook his head. "I mean - I thought -" He rubbed his hand across his brow. "Do we have any idea who this guy is yet? Don't we have any suspects?"

"I put a surveillance team on our most promising suspect," Frankie answered. "I put a call in to 'em when I got here. They say the guy finally showed up at home last night and they followed him to work this morning." He shook his head in frustration. "They said he hasn't left work all day. Unless he found a way to lose them, I'd say he's not our guy after all, so, no, we don't know who we're dealing with. It's all going to come down to what Neil can tell us, and the forensics. I just hope this guy is in the system."

Noah took a seat next to Frankie, and they all lapsed into silence, everyone's attention devoted to watching the clock and the doorway. Eventually, Conrad decided to take the time to deliver the evidence to the lab, but came back straight away less than half an hour later. Robin knew he needed to be there when Neil got out of surgery - regardless of the result - to document his injuries and collect any other evidence there may be. But, most importantly, she knew he needed to be there for his partner and best friend. But when he got back, there was still no word from the doctors.

At one point, Noah jumped up and rushed out into the hall to intercept a tall, handsome older man in a fine suit and an elegant, dark-haired woman in a stylish ensemble who, from the strong resemblance, she guessed were Neil's parents. Conrad joined them and they all spoke at length, occasionally putting a hand on one's shoulder or offering other such gestures. Robin suddenly felt out of place.

"I'm gonna check in with the lab," she muttered to Frankie, slipping out to the payphones. She called Tyler's extension.

"A/V lab, Hendricks."

"Hey, Ty. It's Robin."

"Hey, what's up?"

"I was just checking up on you. How's it going?"

"I was able to conclusively rule out Franks' prime suspect. So I guess we're back to square one."

"Yeah, well, he just said a little while ago that he checked in with the team sitting on him and they haven't seen him leave work all day."

"Wait – are you at the hospital, too?"

"Uh, yeah. I took a couple of hours off." Her cheeks flushed. She knew it must look a little odd for her to be here, since she hadn't worked with Neil as long as Tyler and the others. But the pathetic truth was these guys were the only friends she had in this city, and over the last few months she had grown especially fond of Neil. "I just wanted to make sure he's going to be all right."

"How's it looking?"

"We don't know yet. He's in surgery."

"Oh. Was there anything else I can do for you?"

"No, just checking." She lowered her voice. "Actually, I just wanted to be doing something. The waiting is stressing everybody out way too much. Neil's parents are here now – and Harkham, man," she blew out a breath. "Seeing them going through this is breaking my heart."

"Yeah, it's things like this that make me grateful we get to stay in the lab, you know? I feel bad for Parker and the others sometimes," his voice trailed off. "Hey, Shots, I think I've got something here."

"What?"

"I just spotted a guy on one of the department store's surveillance tapes buying scrubs like the ones the attacker wore at the hospital. I gotta take a closer look and run him through the facial recognition software, but I'm already 99.9 percent sure it's our guy. I gotta go, but I'll page you when I get the results."

"Okay," she said just before he hung up. She slipped back into the waiting room where Noah and Neil's parents were now seated closely together on another small couch, talking quietly. She caught Conrad's attention and gestured for him to join her in talking to Frankie. She didn't care what was going on between them at the moment, her announcement was more important.

"Tyler's got a lead for you," she told them. "He's found footage of a guy he's pretty sure is the killer buying the scrubs he wore to the hospital. Apparently he's got a decent face shot because he's says he's running him through the facial recognition software. He's gonna page us with the results."

"So it's definitely not Walt McMurty?"

"That's your prime suspect? Then no, he says he was able to rule him out. This is someone you haven't looked at yet."

"Okay. Thanks, Shots," he favored her with a lopsided grin. He then turned a serious mien to Conrad. "If we get a location before he comes out of surgery, have Branson and a nurse in there when you process and interview him. I wanna make sure I'm there to bring this guy down."

CHAPTER TWENTY-NINE

―――――

"NOAH?" AUNT HELEN ASKED. "What is it?"

They were now seated on one of the long sofas, and he was watching Frankie and the others huddled together talking. He looked back at his aunt and gestured toward the group. "I know that look. Frankie's waiting to roll on something. The lab must've turned something up." He chafed the palm of his bandaged hand on his thigh and drummed the fingers of his other hand on the sofa's arm rest.

Uncle Michael leaned forward, looking past his wife at him. "Can they tell us what they know? Can you find out what it is?"

It physically hurt to see the fear and worry in their faces, but he was as much an outsider now as they were. "Uncle Michael, I'm not a cop anymore. I can't find out anything more than what they could tell you." And yet they still looked at him with wet, hopeful eyes. "But why don't I try anyway?"

He got up and picked his way around the scattered coffee tables and chairs. The group fell silent at his approach. "Frankie? What is it? Do you have a suspect?"

Frankie exchanged a look with the others as if getting a group consensus. They all nodded. He turned back to Noah. "We have a suspect, but are waiting on an ID and address. We don't know anything definite yet."

"Okay. When you do, you'll let me know, right?" Frankie nodded and Noah gave him a small smile. "Good. Thanks, partner." He was going to make sure he was there when Frankie took this guy down.

CHAPTER THIRTY

"Without pain, there would be no suffering, without suffering we would never learn from our mistakes. To make it right, pain and suffering is the key to all windows, without it, there is no way of life."

-Angelina Jolie

"THIS IS BEYOND MY ABILITIES, you know that, right?" The old man was looking at him coolly, the downy tufts of white hair highlighted by the bright, bare bulb dangling from the ceiling behind him.

He knew. He had nowhere else to go; nowhere he wouldn't be picked up the moment he was treated. The old man couldn't save him, but he could buy him some time, and it was time he needed. He had already begun to get exhausted by the time he showed up here. The bleeding was stopped now, but the bullet was still imbedded within his shattered bones.

"Even if I can get it out and keep you from bleeding to death – which in itself would be a miracle, mind you – you'd never be able to use that arm properly again. Only surgery can fix it, make it heal the way it should." The old man studied him closely a moment, his tongue protruding slightly from the left corner of his mouth. "I can do nothing more for you. You need a real doctor, not a cut man. I'm sorry, my boy."

He couldn't go to a real doctor, they'd be looking for him already. He felt his eyelids wanting to close. It was a struggle of supreme effort to keep them open, to listen as the old man continued talking. "There is...one person who may be able to help you. It will be difficult, oh yes, to say the least, but I am owed."

136

He began to move about the room, searching for something, speaking as if to himself. "She will have to come here, there's no way around that. Can't be moving you in your condition until she's done. Don't worry, I know a place where you can recover – you can't go home, you know. But she is discreet; we shouldn't have to worry about unwanted guests. Ah, here it is," he said triumphantly, discovering a cell phone under a pile of towels on the low bench.

He half listened as the old man made a strange, cryptic phone call, concentrating on keeping the piece of paper clutched in his bloody right hand. But he could no longer keep his eyes open, and, despite his fear he may never wake up again, he succumbed to unconsciousness.

CHAPTER THIRTY-ONE

———

NEARLY HALF AN HOUR passed since Robin had spoken to Tyler and over two hours since Neil had been taken up to surgery. Robin and Officer Branson had located a vending area and brought sodas, candy bars and chips back to those waiting, hoping to make the time pass more quickly. Noah stayed near his aunt and uncle, offering what comforting words he could manage. Robin stayed near Conrad but Frankie and Branson kept mostly to themselves, though one of them often made attempts to get an update on Neil's condition.

At long last, a weary doctor came to the waiting room, doffing the cap he'd been wearing to cover his hair. "Mr. and Mrs. Coates?" His eyes searched the group and settled on the couple.

They rose to their feet, Noah with them. "Yes?" Michael's voice shook as he took his wife's hand in his.

The doctor looked around the room. "If you'd like to step outside here with me a moment," he gestured for them to accompany him.

The others exchanged anxious glances and watched the three of them step out into the hall with the surgeon. They watched with bated breath as the doctor spoke in words too quiet to hear, relying on the family's reaction to answer the question on everybody's mind.

Helen turned her face toward her husband, burying it against his chest and sobbing. Robin felt her blood go cold.

Then, Michael smiled.

Noah shook hands with the surgeon and hugged his aunt and uncle. Then he came into the waiting room, looking ready to collapse from relief. "He's alive."

"Thank God," Shots said and Conrad asked, "How is he – when can we see him?"

"He's being taken to a room. You'll get to see him first to process him, but he...they had to intubate him. The tube is still down his throat, so he won't be able to talk." He reached out a hand to find the nearest chair and lowered himself to sit on the arm of it. His hands were trembling again.

"They had to transfuse over a fourth of his blood volume during the surgery. They said the glass nicked the carotid artery and several veins. If he hadn't prevented that guy from pulling the glass back out, he, uh...he would've died right there at the scene."

A tear slid down his face and he wiped it away with the heel of his hand. "The doctor said, as it was, he arrested on the operating table twice. They almost couldn't bring him back. He's going up to ICU for now, but they think he'll be fine. Weak for a while, of course, but fine."

Helen came in and put a hand on Noah's shoulder. "He's in a room now. The nurse said Conrad and the Detective can see him first, then we can sit with him." She gave Conrad a warm smile.

"We'll be quick about it, Helen," Conrad assured her.

Robin's pager beeped and everyone turned their eyes to her. She looked down and announced, "It's Tyler." She looked at Frankie.

He nodded and rushed out of the room.

CHAPTER THIRTY-TWO

———

FRANKIE EXCUSED HIMSELF and went to the payphone and called the A/V lab number. "Tyler, it's Detective Franks. Tell me you've got him."

"Joseph Anthony Barrett," Tyler announced. "Served five years in Boston when he was eighteen for setting abandoned cars on fire. Moved here about nine years ago. Arrested four years ago for second degree arson on the south side, but he was released after serving only eight months. His current address is the Ruby Motel on Queen Street."

"That's less than a mile from Brookview," he muttered. "Okay, thanks, Tyler. Have you spoken to Parker yet?"

"Not yet."

"Okay, I'll give him a call. Neil just got out of surgery. They think he's going to be all right. Let everyone know for me?"

"Excellent," Tyler replied. "Yes, I will. See you Frankie."

"Thanks, see ya." Frankie hung up and immediately made another call, this time to Parker. "Cal, it's Franks. Tyler got our guy. Joseph Anthony Barrett; lives on Queen Street at the Ruby Motel. How soon can you get there?"

"I'm about twenty minutes away from that side of town. I'm taking the evidence from Harkham's place back to the lab. I can meet you there in about half an hour."

"Okay. I'll get the warrant and have Cox and Adelmo meet us there, too."

"Great. I'm on my way. Any word on Neil?"

"He's out of surgery, in the ICU. They say he's going to be okay."

"Thank God," he said.

"Yeah. But this guy is still a murderer – whatever it takes, we get him. Today."

"We'll get him. I'll see you in thirty minutes."

"Right. Thanks, Cal." He hung up. When he turned around, Noah was standing in front of him.

"I'm coming with you."

"What? Hark – no, I can't do that. I can't take a - a -"

"A civilian to track down a suspect? Frankie, it's me – I may not be your partner anymore, but I am hardly a civilian. I'm coming with you."

Frankie tried to walk past him, but Noah stopped him with a hand on his chest. "This is insane, Noah!" he whispered fiercely. "You know how it works – I cannot take you with me. Besides, this guy already thinks he killed you once, what makes you think he won't do it again?"

Noah shrugged. "So give me a vest, but I owe it to Neil to be there when you catch this guy. Besides, like you said, he's already killed me once – what better to stop him dead in his tracks than to see me coming at him? I can help you. You know I can."

"Maybe, maybe not. If this goes south and turns to chaos - like it probably will - how are you gonna see this guy creeping up on you out of the shadows? Look, I'm sorry, but come on, man, you know this can't happen. I mean, if you couldn't even -" He stopped himself and ran a hand over his mouth.

"Say it," Noah ordered. "If I couldn't even what?"

Frankie stared him down a moment, but then sighed. "It won't be like in Ziehring's office out there. It won't nearly be as good of conditions. Plus," he lowered his voice, "when I got here and you came out of the waiting room to meet me, you walked into the coffee table, man, like you didn't even know it was there. If you couldn't," he paused, hating to speak to his best friend this way.

"If you couldn't see that, and you couldn't hear me coming up behind you in a small, quiet room..." He shook his head. "Hark, I'm sorry, but I could get written up just for having this conversation with you."

Noah had waited, his expression unreadable, through all this, but now he squared his shoulders and took a step forward with a look of determination. "I can do this, Frankie. I'm not some poor disabled kid you have to babysit, all right? I saw the guy, I can -"

"You said all you saw was his arm."

"And I know exactly where I shot it. You're not going to find him easily. Let me help you. He's too smart to go home; you'll be wasting your time at the Ruby."

"It's the only lead we've got so far. It's just a place to start, that's all."

"I think I may know of a better one," a voice behind Noah said. The two looked and found Robin Dorian standing there. "And I actually think Detective Harkham might come in handy."

"What are you getting at, Shots?"

"If you come up empty at the Ruby," she hesitated, flicking a glance at Noah, "go back and talk to Bobby Avalon."

"What?" Noah asked. "What's he got–"

"Absolutely not," Frankie firmly declared. "You're crazier than he is if you think I'm going to let those two anywhere near each other."

"I think he knows a lot more than he's saying. Avalon's a boxer; he's not easily bullied. But after what he did to Harkham, he's likely to sing like a bird if he sees him coming after him."

Noah nodded to her. "She's right, Frankie. This could be our only shot." When Frankie didn't reply right away, he leaned in and lowered his voice to say, "I have to see this through. Please."

Frankie's gaze shifted between Robin and Noah as he tried to think of a better alternative to her reckless plan. "What about when Neil asks why you aren't here?"

"He'll understand," Noah said evenly. "He'll get why I have to do this."

Frankie turned to Robin. "We don't even know for sure Bobby Avalon has anything to do with this. The only connection we have is his gun, which he claims was stolen."

She dipped her head, conceding. "Yes, but, as Parker says, that doesn't mean it really was stolen. Maybe he gave it to Barrett. All I'm saying is run whatever checks you have to run and go through his apartment - but if you don't find what you need, then talk to Avalon." She eyed him. "It's worth a try, isn't it?"

He considered it another long moment. "I can't believe I'm doing this," he whispered. He turned to Noah. "You will be wearing body armor at all times and you will do exactly as I say. It's my badge and both our lives on the line, you got it?" Noah nodded in agreement. "I'll check the Ruby - you'll stay in the car - then we pay a visit to Mr. Avalon if we have to."

Noah nodded. "All right."

"Hark, I'm serious, man. You have to play this to the letter - one wrong move and he'll either try to kill us or have us arrested. Do you copy?"

"I copy, Frankie."

He sighed. "Right. Let's go; Cal and the others will be waiting."

Noah turned to Robin. "Shots, will you tell my aunt and uncle I -"

"I've got this, you go," she told him with a smile.

He clapped her on the shoulder and headed toward the elevator. Frankie paused on his way past. "This is either a brilliant idea or a terrible one," he told her.

She winked. "Have faith."

CHAPTER THIRTY-THREE

―――

"THERE WAS SIGNIFICANT swelling," the nurse informed them as Ward and Branson stood outside the door to Neil's room. "The paramedics had to intubate him to keep his airway open, and we'll have to leave it in until the swelling goes down again." She glanced inside the room. "It looks like he's starting to wake up. You can go in, but try to be quick. Writing will be very tiring for him, so try to keep your questions to the minimum. Okay?"

"Yes, ma'am," Conrad answered her. She nodded and led them into the room. Neil lay in the bed with a multitude of wires and tubes connecting him to various machines, each of which emitted some sort of beep or other sound. A large plastic tube protruded from between his lips.

Conrad's stomach felt like someone had dropped a huge, cold stone into the pit of it and tears burned at the back of his eyes. Neil's eyelids fluttered and he opened them slowly. "Hey, there," Conrad said.

Neil shifted his eyes toward him and tried to say something. "No, no," Conrad cautioned, "don't talk, okay? They had to put a tube down your throat, so just relax for a bit, yeah?"

Neil nodded, the large gauze bandage on his throat making the movement stiff and slow. He lifted his uninjured left hand, which was curled into a tight ball, and carefully opened it. "Did you get epithelials?" Conrad asked.

Neil nodded and Conrad quickly got out the collection kit and began to scrape under Neil's fingernails, collecting the skin cells trapped under them. "You're a lucky son, you know that? You scared us all to death," Conrad told him. "I didn't like it." He couldn't tell for sure, but it looked like Neil quirked the corner of his mouth in a slight, ironic smile.

Officer Branson took out his notebook and pen and came to the side of Neil's bed as Conrad stepped back. Branson placed the pen in Neil's left hand and held the notebook in front of him. The injured criminalist didn't wait for a question – he began to write immediately and with great effort. When he was finished he looked at Branson.

Branson looked at what was written. "He says, 'he said sorry, someone had to pay.'" He looked at Neil. "The attacker said this?" Neil nodded. "When? Before or after he stabbed you?" Neil made a gesture with the pen. "After," Branson translated.

"What kind of perp apologizes to someone he thinks he's going to kill?" Ward asked with a frown.

"We'll find out," Branson answered. "Neil – did you get a good look at the guy at all? Do you remember his clothes, build, hair color or anything?" At Neil's gesture, he put the notebook closer to his hand. Neil wrote slowly, and Branson read the words off as each was written. "Five-five or six...one sixty-ish...35 to 45...dark hair, graying...didn't see face...black jacket, hat with Gianni's logo –" he stopped reading and looked at Conrad. "Gianni's?"

"Pizza place just up the block from Harkham's apartment."

Branson continued to read. "...had accent...familiar."

"The guy sounded familiar?" Conrad asked. Neil nodded. "Like maybe from an old case?" Neil made a vague gesture with his hand that Ward interpreted as a maybe. "Okay, what kind of accent was it? Did he sound foreign?"

Neil wrote and Branson read off, "'Chicago...Boston.' And he's got a question mark after that."

Conrad looked at Branson with a slight eyebrow shrug. "I'll check with Frankie," he told him. "Neil, Frankie thinks we know who this guy is. Maybe you've had a run-in with him before – Joseph Anthony Barrett?"

Neil thought a long moment, looking exhausted. The nurse, who had kept quiet and out of the way so far, stepped a little closer and eyed his monitors uneasily. Neil gave her a look, and she seemed convinced he was okay...for now. Suddenly, Neil's eyes widened a bit and he wrote something.

"He says, 'J. Anthony Barrett equals Tony.' Now he's writing 'Woodbridge.'" Branson waited while Neil slowly wrote more. "He wrote a Q apostrophe D, so, uh, I guess questioned?" Neil gave him a thumbs up. "Okay, now I-N-S period E-V period."

"Insufficient evidence," Conrad supplied, remembering. "That's right. Tony Barrett – I remember him now. You liked him for the Woodbridge Center fire – insurance fraud deal a few years back –" he added for Branson's benefit, "but there wasn't enough evidence to prove it was him, so he got off." He and Neil exchanged a look. "Neil, Tyler's pretty sure he's our guy. Can you confirm?"

Neil nodded his head slightly. Branson read what he slowly wrote next. "He says, 'could be, need to hear.'"

"Okay, that's good." He put a hand on Neil's shoulder. "Thank you, man. I've got to take some photos now, so just try to relax – pretend you're a model."

Neil wrote something and tilted it toward Conrad, who laughed when he read it. "He's wondering if he'll make it into the ICU pin-up calendar," he informed the nurse. Although she and Branson both laughed, her eyes kept close watch on Neil and his monitors.

She frowned. "You're going to have to wrap this up, gentlemen. He needs to rest."

Conrad photographed the bandages around Neil's right hand, from where the mirror's sharp edges had left deep lacerations on his fingers as he held onto it, then took pictures of the bandage on his neck and a general overall shot. "I'll need to photograph the wounds themselves," he informed the nurse. "Will I be able to do that or...?"

The nurse pursed her lips thoughtfully and eyed the clock. "I suppose I could go ahead and change them a little early. I don't want to expose the wounds long, I don't want to risk infection."

Conrad nodded and he and Branson backed out of her way. She moved with confident efficiency, removing the bandage from his hand first. Neil winced and stifled a groan when she straightened his fingers enough for them to see the stitches on his fingers and palm. The cuts were deep, the skin red and swollen still. Man, the pain would be unbearable, if it weren't for the painkillers they were giving him.

Conrad snapped a few quick photos, then nodded to her. "Sorry, bro," he muttered to Neil.

She put a new bandage on the hand and moved on to his neck. This one took less time to uncover and was more easily seen. It looked less painful than the ones on his hand, but that was only because the majority of the damage was below the surface. He took several photographs and then backed away with a sympathetic look at his best friend. "You're good to go now, man."

"Okay, then I guess that's all we need here for now," Branson said, pocketing his notebook and pen. He gave Neil a reassuring smile. "Take it easy, Coates."

Neil weakly gripped the officer's hand in parting, then did the same with Conrad's. As they started to leave, Ward turned back and said, "By the way, you should have come up with a better excuse to avoid the hearing. Parker would say we can just use your monitors in place of a polygraph." Neil's mouth twitched.

"Your folks are here, and Harkham, of course. Shots is out there, too, and the others will be by as soon as they can." He could feel a lump forming in his throat and did his best to ignore it. "We were all pulling for ya. Take care of yourself, man. I'll see you soon." He squeezed Neil's arm and he and Branson left, leaving the nurse to her patient once more.

Once outside in the hallway, Conrad leaned against the wall and put his face in his hands. He took a couple of deep breaths and let them out slowly. Branson dipped his head to look him in the eye. "You okay?"

Conrad raked his fingers through his hair and gave the officer a weak smile. "Yeah," he said. "It just kinda hit me, how close it came. I mean, I've never seen this guy even sick a single day in the six years I've known him, and so this? Yeah, this was scary."

"He's going to be fine. You heard what they said. Right?" His words sounded confident, but his eyes looked worried, scared.

"Okay, yeah, thanks. What about you? You look pretty shaken up by all this. Do you know him well?"

"Me? Oh, no, not really." He shrugged, but the gesture looked forced. "I guess it's just the thought that it might've been any one of us he came after... You know?"

"Yeah. This whole thing is pretty messed up, huh?"

Branson smiled, and tapped the back of his hand on Conrad's arm. "Why don't you get this stuff to the lab and I'll see how we can help the others find this guy?"

CHAPTER THIRTY-FOUR

———

"The dead cannot cry out for justice. It is a duty of the living to do so for them."

- Lois McMaster Bujold

HE CAME TO IN A LOW-lit room, a different one than he had fallen asleep in. His mouth was dry and his head swam. Laying still, he assessed his condition a moment before realizing he didn't feel any pain. Gently, he touched his fingers to his left arm, moving it up toward the shoulder. His arm was in a cast from the elbow up to his neck, a sling cradling the limb against his body. He lifted his head and saw he was lying on a bed in what appeared to be someone's apartment, but he didn't recognize it. His body felt limp and leaden, but his heart pounded joyfully - he was alive!

Movement to his right caught his eye and he slowly reached for the .38, which he was surprised to find lying next to him. The click of the hammer pulling back made the figure freeze. "Please," the woman said in a careful, calming tone, "I'm only here to check on you."

Her voice was vaguely familiar and he remembered the cut man mentioning a woman he thought could help.

"You're extremely lucky I was able to see you. If I hadn't gotten the bullet out and screwed those bones in the right place, you would be in a very bad way right now."

He returned the hammer to the non-firing position carefully and laid the gun down.

"If you ask me," she continued, coming closer, "if you had only used that to begin with, you wouldn't have needed me."

He ignored her commentary and groaned as the room began to spin. He closed his eyes but the sensation remained. She laid a hand on his forehead, then took his pulse in his throat and left wrist. Once the room stood still again, he opened his eyes and got his first look at her. He estimated her age to be around forty and she had thin, sharp features that could have been harsh and hawkish, but had somehow turned out elegant, if not pretty. Her black hair was cropped short and stylish and she wore scrubs under a lab coat.

"My uncle told me about you," she said, her face leaning close to his as she examined his eyes with a small penlight. He tried not to blink as she flicked the light across his line of vision multiple times. "This is all his world, not mine - and I wouldn't have come if I didn't owe him." She put down the penlight. "When I leave here I don't know you and you don't know me. I don't ever want to see you again, understand? If anyone ever found out I helped you..."

He swallowed thickly, his tongue sandpaper against the roof of his mouth. She picked up a cup of water he hadn't noticed on the nightstand and placed the straw in his mouth. When he had drunk his fill he asked her if she was a doctor. She gave a low, throaty laugh. "Veterinarian," she replied simply.

She began collecting her things from around the room. "There's an opening in the cast for you to change the bandage on the entry wound and incisions. On the nightstand are a bottle of antibiotics and painkillers - enough for six weeks, which is when the cast can come off. It'll be up to you to manage that. You lost a lot of blood and I don't have access to human blood to replace it with, which is why you feel so dizzy and weak. It will pass, especially once you've started eating again, and you should feel right as rain in a couple of days. The cooler on the chair over here has food and water in it. Your money, minus the cost of supplies, is under the bed."

He didn't need to ask to know she found what she had done for him distasteful and he wondered what kind of favor the cut man had done for her to earn such a favor in return. He told her to take an additional twenty grand out of the bag to give her uncle. A final payment, he called it. She took it out and stuffed it into her medical bag, handling it like a venomous snake.

He smiled to himself. At least he didn't need to worry about her keeping it for herself. The only thing he did worry about was whether or not she might decide to call in an anonymous tip once she was far away from here.

"Just out of curiosity," she was saying as she laid her hand on the door handle, "why did you do it? Why stab the crime scene investigator if you'd already killed the nurse? Why do any of this?"

He frowned. He didn't kill the nurse. It was the retired cop, the one Avalon almost put down, that he killed. There was no crime scene investigator. He told her she must have gotten her information mixed up.

She looked at him like she wondered if she gave him the wrong meds. "The news said the nurse died this morning and that you'd stabbed a crime scene investigator and put him in the ICU. There was no mention of a cop, retired or otherwise. They've been running a press conference clip of the detective on your case. He said you were clever, but ultimately a failed serial killer. Is that what this is? Are you a serial killer?"

His mind raced; conflicting emotions roiled in his gut. The media must have been misinformed, he insisted.

"Maybe, maybe not." She shrugged. "But you still haven't answered my question: why have you done all this?"

"Because they failed," he said. "Just like I did."

CHAPTER THIRTY-FIVE

———

NOAH GLANCED OUT THE window of Frankie's Chrysler and then checked his watch again. "You're wasting time," he grumbled, adjusting his Kevlar vest. Barrett wasn't here, he could feel it, and this delay was costing precious time. But Frankie had to go through protocol, he supposed. He just hoped it would yield something useful.

If he could just go inside, instead of being stuck in the car like a child. Maybe Parker would tell him what he found, one forensic scientist to another...but probably not. He detected movement and saw Frankie and the others leaving the building. Parker loaded up the evidence bags he carried out and Cox and Adelmo got in their cruiser. Frankie waited until they left before approaching the car.

"Finally," he muttered with a sigh as Frankie opened the door. "Well? How did it go? What did you find?"

Frankie buckled his seat belt. "Not much," he said, starting the car. "There were some newspaper articles saved in a file Parker found under the mattress. All about Brookview." He pulled out of the lot and into the flow of traffic. "But we didn't find the Colt or the scrubs."

"So we go talk to Avalon now?"

Frankie glanced over at him. "It's thin, Hark. We'll only be able to ask a few questions, we don't have enough to hold him on anything."

"Not yet," he said, lifting one eyebrow. "That's the whole point of this little excursion."

"Fishing expedition," Frankie scoffed. But he continued on toward Avalon's apartment anyway.

It was good being back in this car with Frankie. Even though it was a one-off thing, it still felt like nothing had changed. At least for the moment.

"So do you remember this Barrett guy?"

Noah nodded. "I do, yeah. He was what you might call Neil's white whale. Barrett was brought in for questioning in connection to the Woodbridge Center fire. It was Wilkerson's case, not mine, but Neil was talking to me about it one day. He said everyone knew Barrett was guilty, but he didn't find enough evidence to prove it. That's why the allegations against him in the Turner case couldn't be dismissed so easily. Some think he'd do anything to keep that from happening again. Which is total BS."

He fell silent a few seconds. "But what I don't understand is why," he continued. "I mean, what's his motive? I thought we were looking for someone who lost someone in the Brookview fire. How does Barrett fit in?"

Frankie shrugged. "That's just one of the things I plan to find out when I get him into an interrogation room."

Noah chewed all this over another minute, before his thoughts took another tack. "So where's your new partner been for all this?"

Frankie flicked him a confused look. "New partner?"

"Yeah. It's been nearly a year, Ziehring'd have to have you partnered up by now."

"I work solo most of the time, actually. Once in a while, I'll back up one of the others if need be." He scratched at a spot along his jaw. "I worked a case with Townsend last month. Homicide on the north end. The girl that was found in the retention pond with a broken neck."

"Townsend, huh? He's pretty good, I suppose. I don't remember hearing much about that one - did you close it?"

"Yeah. Turned out to be accidental, she fell down the stairs at her boyfriend's house. But the boyfriend freaked out and dumped her body in the pond to make it look like someone killed her." He gave him a bleak grin and shook his head. "The parents were out of town and he was supposed to be in boarding school...anyway, he didn't want anyone to find out they were alone in his parent's place. Stupid."

"Yeah. What happened to him?"

"It's still tied up in court. Will be for quite a while, probably. Both families are insanely rich and they're both trying to buy a verdict, in my opinion."

"Hmm, the legal system at its finest."

They pulled into the parking lot for Avalon's building. Noah felt a sudden shiver of anxiety at seeing the boxer again, and finally had to admit to himself Frankie's objections to this risky proposition were legitimate. But he was determined that, whatever Avalon tried to throw at him, he was going to handle this as if it were any other case.

Frankie turned off the car, then turned to Noah with a serious expression. "Are you sure about this?"

"Yes." Zero hesitation.

Frankie nodded, looking resigned. "In that case, open the glove compartment."

Noah gave him an odd look, but did as he bid anyway. There was a gun inside. Noah picked it up and, as soon as he had it in hand, felt a shock of recognition. The grip nestled into his palm and his wrist took the weight as if not a single day had passed. It was his gun, the Springfield XD he'd carried every day his entire career. "Where did you get this?" he asked, almost in awe. "I thought you had gotten rid of it."

"I've been holding onto it since - for a long time."

Noah knew what it meant for Frankie to have given the gun back, in light of what it had meant when he took it away. Unbidden, memories from a day not long after Avalon ended Noah's career flitted through his mind. It was the darkest point of his life, and it had nearly come to a violent end on that night, if not for Frankie. It was something he tried not to think about anymore, and he was grateful Frankie wasn't getting into it now. "Thanks," he managed to say.

Frankie gave him a sort of sad smile. "Yeah. But it's only to be used if absolutely necessary, okay? And, for the record, you don't have that and I never gave it to you, got it?"

Noah nodded. "Got it."

"Okay, let's get this over with," Frankie said, getting out of the car.

Noah got out and slid the gun into the waist band of his athletic pants at his hip and made sure his old 'Police Dept.' shirt covered it. He then followed his old partner into the building and up to Avalon's apartment. He stayed to the left of the door and waited while Frankie knocked. There was no reply. Frankie pounded on it, but, again, no response.

"Now what?" Noah asked.

Frankie blew out a breath and thought a moment. He looked at his watch and his expression changed, like an idea had sprung to mind. "Last time we were here Avalon said he was on his way to the ring. It was about this time of day," he said, digging out his cell phone. "What do you want to bet he's there now?" He made a call to the precinct and got the address of Avalon's boxing ring. He thanked the clerk and hung up. "One more try."

———————————

FRANKIE PULLED INTO the lot servicing the ring where Bobby Avalon now instructed the local thugs in the way of the glove. There were no other cars yet, but the lights were on inside. "You ready?" Frankie asked, switching off the ignition.

Noah took a breath. "Ready."

"Remember, don't let this guy get under your skin. If you cross the line, Ziehring will have you behind bars and me up before Internal Affairs so fast we won't see it coming."

"I get it. It's only been nine months, I haven't forgotten how to be a cop."

"I know that, but this is different." He looked like he was going to say more, but Noah stared him down. "Fine. Let's just get in there and get this done."

They got out of the car and Noah let Frankie lead the way to the training grounds of future champions. He peered in through the window as they got to the entrance. "I don't see anybody," he announced. "No bystanders, which is good. Let's see if we can find the Mallet himself."

The smell of stale sweat, canvas and old blood hit them the moment they went through the door. To their left was an empty room labeled 'First Aid.' To the right, another empty room was labeled 'Manager's Office - Employees Only.' Across the big open room, past punching bags, mats, racks of free weights and the ring itself, was a locker room entrance.

Frankie double checked and cleared the two side rooms, then went to the locker room entrance, hugging his back to the wall and glanced inside. "Hello? Is anyone here?"

"Be right with ya, pal," a gruff voice from the back of the locker room replied.

Noah, who had dropped back out of sight behind a support column near the ring, felt his body go cold at the sound of that voice. He tensed. "It's him," he whispered, his heart rate increasing. "It's Avalon."

Frankie nodded and motioned for him to stay out of sight. After a few moments, Bobby Avalon came out of the locker room wearing track pants and a tee shirt. His skin was damp and he had a towel draped across his shoulders. He took one look at Frankie and froze. "What are you doing here? Looking for a lesson or two?"

"Actually, my partner and I have a few questions for you, Avalon." He gestured toward Noah, who stepped out of the shadow to lean against the column, his shirt rearranged to display the gun at his hip.

Avalon went pale, but then put on a tough act. "Partner, huh? Well, I know you're not trying to pass him off as a cop, cuz I know they had to put him out to pasture."

"And yet, here I am," Noah said, fighting the urge to wipe the smugness off the boxer's face. "I think you should be praying I'm here - armed - on police business, because after what you did to me, well..." he shrugged, then took a sudden step toward Avalon.

The boxer retreated a few steps and found himself backed up against the ring, with Noah on one side and Frankie on his other, blocking the path to the door. "What is this, huh?" He jerked his thumb toward Frankie. "You send your little sidekick away and how 'bout you and I settle this like men: inside the ring."

Noah took a few more steps closer. "All we want is information. You tell us where Tony Barrett is and we'll leave."

"Is that right? Well, what if I told you I don't know who or what you're talking about?" Avalon put a few inches between himself and the ring and rolled his shoulders.

"Then I'd say you should think a little harder."

He appeared to be considering this, then a maliciousness spread across his face. "Yeah, all right. He's in there," he said, jutting his left hand to Noah's right, toward the locker room. Reflexively, Noah shifted his eyes, trying to keep the boxer's hand in sight. Avalon threw a right hook, connecting hard with the exposed left side of Noah's face.

Noah staggered back with a groan, more from anger than pain, though it did ring his bell. He looked back up to see Avalon slip around the corner of the ring, and Frankie drawing his gun. "Avalon, stop! Freeze!" Frankie ordered. He eased to the other side of the ring, placing himself between the ring and the exit. He spared Noah a glance and mouthed, 'You okay?'

Noah wiped blood from his nose and cheek and nodded. He drew his gun, too and watched Frankie for his cue.

"That was a dirty, underhanded thing to do, Bobby," Frankie said, inching toward the back of the ring. "If that's the way you used to play it in the ring, no wonder they made you hang up your gloves." He peeked around the back corner of the ring, but ducked back to motion to Noah where Avalon was hiding.

"Then why don't you put on a pair and show me how it's done, Detective," Avalon said, a sneer in his voice. "Now that our little friend is taking a nap."

Noah circled around toward the back of the ring from the opposite side from Frankie. "Now, now, Bobby," he said, "what kind of guy do you think I am that I'd let a jelly fisted punch like that put me down, huh? They should've called you the Rubber Mallet."

Noah rounded the corner to face Avalon. The boxer was in the middle of putting on a pair of boxing gloves from a rack behind the ring. "Don't move, Bobby."

Over his shoulder, Noah saw Frankie come up behind Avalon with his gun trained on the back of his head. "Put down the gloves, Bobby, and then put your hands up." He followed the boxer's movements with his gun as he complied. "All we want is information. If you cooperate, you may get a fair shake. If you don't, you'll go down for assault and possibly even accessory to murder."

Avalon stayed put but turned his head toward Frankie. "Hey, I didn't kill anybody!"

Frankie ignored him. "If you run or attack either of us again, I will have no choice but to use deadly force to defend myself and my partner. You got all that?" He waited until Avalon nodded, the boxer never taking his hate-filled eyes off Noah. "Now, like I said, we just need information, so we're gonna sit like civilized adults and talk, right, Bobby?"

Frankie put his hand on the boxer's shoulder, readying to cuff him. But Avalon shrugged him off and lunged at Noah instead. Just like before, Noah couldn't take a shot without endangering someone, but this time, he was ready for it. He sidestepped to the right and used one hand and one foot to redirect Avalon's momentum, sending him sprawling onto the floor. He then grabbed him by the collar and dragged him to his feet, slamming him against another support column.

Noah put his gun to Avalon's head, holding him against the column with his other hand. "Where is Tony Barrett? He came to you, didn't he? His old pal, the guy that gave him the Colt so he could rob those convenience stores and shoot that fireman. Tell me where he is and I might just forget you lost control of your fist."

Frankie closed the distance between them. "Harkham," he said in a warning.

"Wait, Tony stole my Colt?" Avalon looked at him in confusion.

"Stole, borrowed," Noah shrugged. "Whatever you want to call it."

"I didn't give him that gun, I swear! It was stolen. I told your people that."

"Where is Barrett? Where did he go after he came to you?"

"I don't know what you're -" Noah pressed the muzzle of his gun harder against Avalon's temple, causing him to try to squirm away. "All right, all right, all right - he was here. He was bleeding all over my gym. I told him to get out and go to a hospital. There was nothing I could do for him."

Noah glared at him, the man who had ruined his life. He would never get another opportunity like this. He could easily do to Avalon what he'd done to him, and call it self-defense...

Frankie wrapped his fingers around Noah's wrist. He was shocked to see his finger was poised on the trigger, so he placed it outside the trigger guard once more. He flicked a glance at Frankie and eased the pressure off the gun a bit with a nod. Frankie let go.

"Do you know what Luminol and phenolphthalein are, Bobby?" When the boxer didn't answer, Noah went on to explain. "They detect blood, even if someone tried to clean it up. If I search this place, inch by inch, how much of Tony Barrett's blood am I going to find?"

Avalon seemed over his initial fear of Noah's gun, now that Frankie had reined him in, because he sneered again and said, "This is a boxing ring, pal, there's blood everywhere. Besides, I already told you he was here."

"And you said you sent him away, without helping him. So, I shouldn't find his blood on the cut man's exam table, especially not in a quantity that would prove your cut man treated him. Because that would mean you lied to me, and you did aid and abet a criminal - a murderer no less - which makes you an accessory after the fact."

Avalon shrugged as best as he could still pressed against the column. "If my cut man did treat him, it was without my knowledge or consent. You should be talking to him."

"For the sake of argument," Frankie said, "let's say that's true. Then where can we find him? What's his name?"

Avalon shifted his gaze to Frankie. "Everyone calls him Stitch. I don't know his real name."

Noah slammed him against the column again. "He works for you and you're trying to tell me you don't know his name? I know some people who'd be more than happy to comb through your books and employment records, you know, see if they can't find that out for you."

Avalon smiled. "Go ahead. He's paid in cash and all our records are kept by some bookkeeping company."

"And let me guess," Noah said, "you don't know the name of the company either. Bob and Weave, is that it?"

"Like I told your friends, a boxer's memory ain't too reliable." He kept grinning.

Frankie put his gun away, reaching for his cuffs again. "And all those blows to the head musta made you pretty stupid, too, because otherwise you'd realize that by giving up your cut man, you'd be saving yourself some jail time. You could let him take the fall for you instead."

Avalon just gave them both a derisive sneer and kept his mouth shut. "Why don't we give him some time to think about it, Frankie?" Noah asked. "I think we could find him a nice, quiet room." He turned to Avalon. "I hope you don't mind that it's pretty small, right around six by eight."

"You can't arrest me, Harkham, you ain't a cop."

"But I am, you idiot," Frankie said with a sigh. "And like I said, I've got you for assault, interfering with a police investigation, aiding and abetting a fugitive, and I'm sure I can always come up with something else." He held up his cuffs.

Avalon's sneer withered. "I give you Barrett, I don't do time?"

"That will be up to the ADA, but I'll see what we can do." Frankie gave Noah a look, and he backed off, slipping the gun back into his waistband. "IF we get Barrett." He took a small tape recorder out from his pocket and switched it on. "So what's it going to be, Avalon? You gonna give us Tony Barrett?"

The boxer considered a moment. "All right. Tony was here, like I said. Sammy Keane - our cut man, goes by Stitch - he looked him over and stopped the bleeding, but Tony, he needed medical help - real help. Stitch told me he knew someone who could help him, but she won't come if anyone but Stitch and Tony was here. So I left. I just came back about twenty minutes before you got here and they were gone. I cleaned the place up and took a shower. That's all I know, I swear."

"How long ago did you last see Tony? How long were you gone?"

"I left a coupla hours ago."

Frankie nodded. "Okay. And this woman? You don't know who she is?"

Avalon emphatically shook his head. "No, I swear, Stitch wouldn't say anything." He glared at Noah and then Frankie. "That much is free. If you want more, you get me a lawyer - and a deal."

————————

WITHIN MINUTES, AVALON was cuffed and on his way to the precinct in the back of a cruiser. Frankie called Parker and asked him to process the gym to verify Avalon's story. They left a uniform officer on scene to secure the gym until he could arrive. They were going to chase down Sammy Keane.

Before they left, however, Frankie got his first aid kit out of the trunk and retrieved a few items to clean up Noah's face. They got in the car and Frankie handed his partner a bottle of peroxide and some cotton balls, which Noah used to clean the small lacerations on his lip and cheek. "Here," Frankie said, handing over a butterfly closure. "For the one on your cheek."

"Thanks," Noah said, using the visor mirror to apply it. "Avalon's not going to walk away from this completely unscathed, is he? I mean, he will do some time, right?"

"That's up to Gerald, like I said," Frankie replied, punching a cold pack and shaking it to activate the chemicals. "Unless you want to go ahead with the assault charge. But the judge might get a little too interested in why you were here in the first place. I guess we just have to wait and see." He handed the pack to Noah. "I doubt your nose is broken, but you'll probably want to ice it anyway."

"Yeah, thanks." Noah took the pack and gingerly pressed it to his face as Frankie pulled to the exit of the lot. "Remind me to thank Shots for this when we get back, by the way," he snarked, putting the gun back in the glove compartment.

Frankie grinned. "Hey, we got a lead out of it," he said, steering his Chrysler into a break in the traffic. "Stop whining, or she just might break out some darts."

Noah chuckled. "Yeah, you're right. Maybe I'll just tell her that her next bottle of whiskey is on me."

CHAPTER THIRTY-SIX

———

"WE'VE GOT A NEGATIVE on the phone," Cox informed Frankie via their two-way radios. Cox and Adelmo were staked out on one side of the building in which Sammy Keane resided, Frankie and Noah were on the other side. "Doesn't mean he's not there, though, just not answering. How's it look over there, any sign?"

"Still quiet," Frankie replied.

"What do you think, Frankie? Give it a few more minutes or go on up?" Adelmo asked.

"Go on up, but wear your earwigs; I want you to tell us everything you see. We'll keep a lookout down here."

"Right. Standby, switching to headsets," Cox said. The line went silent for a moment, then Frankie's radio chirped. "Okay, Franks, we're heading in now. We got a clear line?"

"Yeah, we can hear you just fine," Frankie said, scanning the area with binoculars. When they all first arrived, Frankie told the two uniform officers Noah was consulting on this case. They hadn't seemed too sure about it, but were going along with it. For now. He needed to talk to Ziehring soon, and hope his boss wouldn't chew him a new one for this reckless venture. "How's it look over there?"

"We've got nothing out here - no people, no traffic," Cox reported. "His apartment is dark. No lights on in any of the others, either."

"The whole building looks empty," Adelmo added.

Noah frowned up at the building and saw they were right. "Almost eight o'clock at night and no one has any lights on? Are we sure about the address?"

"It's the one on file with the DMV. Postal service confirmed," Frankie replied, eyeing the building.

"Something doesn't add up," Noah insisted. "I think they should wait for backup."

"I think the place is empty, Harkham," Cox said. "I think he's using it as a false address. Nobody's here - I say we go on in and check it out, just to be sure."

"But it-"

Noah's protest was cut off by the sound of the two cops running up the steps to the building. "Okay," Cox said, "on three. One...two...three!" There was a loud sound as they burst through the door.

"Riverdale PD!" Adelmo announced.

"Nothing," Cox commented.

Frankie peered toward the building. "What do you see?"

"This place should be condemned, if it isn't already," Adelmo said, coughing. "It looks like everybody just got up and left one day. There's furniture everywhere, but like two inches of dust on everything."

"Franks, I got foot prints," Cox reported. "Lots of 'em. Somebody has been here recently."

"How recently?" Noah asked. "How distinct are the tread patterns?"

"Some are really clear, some are covered in dust," Cox said. "The newest ones are probably a few days old, maybe. I'm seeing at least three different tread patterns."

"Are they all the same size?"

"Um...looks like. Yes."

"And they all go upstairs," Adelmo added. They heard a squeak as he mounted the first stair and they winced. The next step emitted a groan as well, but quieter.

"Go slow and stay close to the wall," Noah instructed. "If the stairs have rotted, they'll be weakest in the middle - and I don't want you overlapping the prints."

"Got it, Hark," Adelmo assured him. "I can see the landing," he whispered. "Looks like just two apartments per floor."

The radio went silent.

"Did you hear that?" Cox's voice was barely audible.

If Adelmo answered, they didn't hear him. But after a few more seconds, he whispered, "We can hear someone moving around in one of these first two apartments... There - somebody's definitely in here." Then, to Cox, he said, "You take two, I'll check one. Nice and easy."

There was a moment of tense silence as the cops readied to enter their respective apartments. Then Adelmo and Cox threw open the apartment doors, announcing, "Riverdale Police!"

After a moment, Adelmo called, "One is clear."

Frankie and Noah leaned forward, peering at the windows. They could see the cops' flashlight beams sweeping the interiors of the apartments. Then one light moved from one side of the building toward the other as Adelmo made his way back to Cox.

Then Cox shouted, "Police! Stop right there!"

Frankie got out of the car. Noah tried to follow suit, but Frankie waved him back. "What's happening up there?" Frankie asked, heading toward the building.

They heard Cox make a sharp exhale and say, "Oh, damn - Adelmo, get over here!"

A couple seconds later, they heard Adelmo blow out a breath, too, as if smelling something foul. "What the-?"

"Hit the lights," Cox instructed. Frankie and Noah saw light shine through the windows on their side of the building.

"What is it? What did you find?" Frankie demanded.

He was almost to the door. Noah drummed his fingers on the armrest, wanting to see the scene for himself. But he stayed where he was, listening to it play out over the radio.

"Uh, Frankie," Adelmo said, his voice a little pinched sounding, "we've got an elderly male - maybe seventy-five or eighty."

Cox's voice cut in. "Sir, can you tell me your name?"

Adelmo continued to report, "He's Caucasian, but filthy - I'm thinking he hasn't bathed in weeks and the apartment is just as bad. But not quite as abandoned looking as downstairs, so he's been here for a while."

They could hear a third voice indistinctly in the background. "We're going to need Social Services to meet us at the hospital," Cox said. "He looks malnourished and seems to have some dementia. But, Franks, he's saying his name is Samuel Keane."

CHAPTER THIRTY-SEVEN

ROBIN SAT IN THE WAITING room, flipping pages of a magazine between sips of coffee. It was less than stellar vending machine stuff, but the added sugar and 'creamer' made it drinkable, if not particularly palatable. She had moved on from soft drinks after finishing a cold sandwich in the cafeteria almost an hour ago, once she'd started getting drowsy. Conrad and Branson had left soon after Noah and Frankie had. She had seen Helen and Michael leaving the cafeteria as she went in, but they were in with Neil again now.

The visiting hours for the ICU were broken up into odd segments, at least to her thinking. When Neil had first gotten out of surgery, it was toward the end of one segment, so after Conrad and Branson left, Helen and Michael had only gotten a short time with their son before being asked to leave. Then there was a lull of two hours when no one was allowed to see him. Now, unless Helen and Michael came out of there in the next hour, she would have to come back in the morning. She didn't want to stay long, she just wanted to see him. She just needed to know he was okay.

With a sigh, she closed the three-month old issue of National Geographic and turned on the television again. She flipped through the channels and saw she had just missed the latest episode of the drama series she followed, so she settled for a mystery halfway over on the local public broadcasting station. However, before she could get interested in it, she heard someone tap on the doorframe and enter the room.

"Hello, dear," Helen Coates said, coming to sit in a chair near Robin's. "I'm sorry we haven't had a chance to talk yet. I'm Helen Coates, Neil's mother," she extended her hand to the younger woman.

"Hi, I'm Robin. Dorian," she replied, shaking Helen's hand. "I work with your son at the lab. I'm ballistics."

"Really?" Helen arched her graceful eyebrows in pleasant surprise. "That does sound interesting. Have you known Neil long?"

"Almost a year. But we've only gotten to know each other over the past few months."

"So you're dating."

Robin blushed. "No."

"You don't find my son attractive?"

"It's not that I - I mean, it's not like that. We're just friends." Her face must have been even redder than a cherry tomato, she thought, and the embarrassment from this fact alone made it get even redder.

Helen laughed gently. "I'm sorry, dear. I didn't mean to make you uncomfortable. Neil's asking for you, and I felt it was my duty as his mother to see what kind of girl he was inviting into his room."

"He asked for me?"

Helen tilted her head. "You seem surprised."

"I just wasn't expecting it, is all. Are you sure he meant me?"

"Yes, he wrote your name on a piece of paper. I asked if he meant the lovely young woman with long brown hair and he nodded. So, I've come to fetch you for him. But if you'd rather not -"

"Oh, no - I want to see him. And, thank you," she added, blushing again.

Helen smiled - one much like Neil's and Noah's - and stood up, reaching a hand out to Robin. She took it and allowed the older woman to assist her to her feet. "It's this way," Helen said, leading the way to Neil's room.

Outside his door, Helen stepped to one side. "Do you need anything before we go? Coffee or soda?"

"No, thank you. You're not staying, then?"

She shook her head. "It's been a...long day. I think we all need to get some rest. Will you tell him again we'll be back in the morning?"

"Of course. And I won't keep him awake long. I just wanted to say hi."

"You've been waiting four hours to say hi?" Helen gave her a knowing look. "My son is very lucky to have a friend like you, Robin. Good night, dear." She smiled again and turned away to head down the hallway.

Robin watched her a moment, trying to allow her face time to resume it's normal coloring, before turning back toward the door. Conrad must have told him she was here, otherwise he probably wouldn't have even thought of her. She took a deep breath and stepped into the room.

Her heart almost stopped at the sight of him. Neil looked like a pincushion. And sort of like an octopus. Needles and tubes seemed to spring out of him from every angle. The tube down his throat was connected to more tubes and a machine to monitor his breathing. Wires led from his chest to a heart monitor, which was making a steady, rhythmic beep. Other sounds - whirrs, clicks and buzzes - created layers of sound above the electric white noise of the overhead lights.

He hadn't noticed her yet, his eyes were closed but she could tell he was awake. "Hi," she said, a little more tremulously than she intended.

He looked at her, and she thought it looked like his eyes were smiling. She took a few steps closer and sat in a chair one of his parents had vacated, relieving her shaking legs of their burden. "How are you feeling?"

He lifted a hand and waggled it, as if saying, 'so-so.' Then he waved it toward her questioningly.

"Me? I'm fine," she laughed a little. "Nobody needs to worry about me right now, least of all you." She searched for something else to say. "I met your mom."

He raised an eyebrow.

"She was very nice."

The corner of his mouth twitched.

"What? She was. Very sweet."

He shook his head just a bit. He gestured in a circle around his face then pointed at hers.

"Oh," she said, feeling the blush creep up again. "She's a little...forward, isn't she? She said it was her duty as your mother to see what kind of girl you were asking into your room." She shook her head with an embarrassed little chuckle.

He closed his eyes a moment and then rolled his wrist to turn his palm up. She took it to be an apology.

"Don't worry about it. I like her. You look a lot like her, you know. And Noah. But I guess you guys probably hear that a lot, huh?"

He nodded.

"She said to tell you she and your dad will be back in the morning."

Again, he nodded.

She looked at him a little more closely. His skin was still pale and there was a slight sheen of sweat on his forehead. She heard the beeping of his heart monitor had increased. She frowned. "Are you sure you're all right? I could get someone - the nurse or a doctor," she said, standing. He reached out and laid his hand on her arm. There was something behind his eyes now - pain or fear, she wasn't sure which.

"Okay," she said, sitting again. "But I'll warn you: I'm not great with these one-sided conversations. You're gonna have to step it up and get better so we can have a real conversation again. You got it?"

He nodded once in mock seriousness, but that look in his eyes was still there. He reached toward her again, gesturing to the necklace at her throat. She felt tears burn the backs of her eyes as she took the cross in her fingers. "Yeah, I've been talking to Him a lot today. I'm thinking of giving Him a huge thank you card."

He patted his chest lightly.

"Yeah, I'll give Him one from you, too." She fell silent and regarded him, resting her elbow on the armrest and her chin in her hand. "It truly is a miracle you're alive. You know that, right?"

He nodded. A tear slid free from the corner of his eye and disappeared into his dark hair.

"Well," she said, clearing her throat, "I told you God is awesome. Now you have proof." She was trying to be glib, but knew the situation didn't warrant it. "I can't tell you how relieved I am you're still with us," she added.

He reached out and squeezed her hand, tears falling freely now, and sniffed. Then he put his hands together as if praying and then reached out to her again.

She nodded and took his hand in hers. "Lord God," she began the prayer, "thank you for bringing Neil back to us..." She continued to pray a few minutes longer, and then realized Neil had once more succumbed to his weariness. Then she continued to pray, holding his hand, until the nurse came to tell her visiting hours were over for the day.

CHAPTER THIRTY-EIGHT

"SAMUEL ROBERT KEANE, age eighty-three," Frankie said, addressing the group of uniform officers he had assembled the next morning, "lives at the Warren Street Apartments, number two. We found him last night and, due to the state of neglect he was living in, he is now in the hospital. But we're looking for his son, Samuel *Ryan* Keane, age sixty-two, A.K.A. Sammy the Stitch, or just Stitch." He held up the enlargements of Keane's DMV photo. "He supposedly lives at the same address as his old man, but now he's in the wind."

Noah began passing out copies of the photo. Several of the officers elbowed the ones next to them and made low comments to each other when they caught sight of him and his scars. He pretended not to notice and let Frankie get on with his briefing.

Frankie held up a photo of Tony Barrett, then gave a stack to Noah to hand out. Again, several whispered to each other and threw looks at him as he gave them the photos.

"Our ultimate target is this man: Joseph Anthony Barrett, goes by Tony," Frankie continued. "I have just received confirmation the suspect's blood recovered from the scene of the attack on Neil Coates is a positive match to DNA taken from Barrett's hotel room. But to get to Tony, we need Samuel Keane, who facilitated medical treatment for Barrett after Noah here put a bullet in him to save Neil's life." He put a hand on Noah's shoulder and gave him a look, a mixture of 'ignore them' and 'sorry, man.' Noah nodded and stepped back to sit on the edge of Frankie's desk.

"Sammy the Stitch knows where Barrett is," Frankie said. "We don't expect him to go back to his father's house - looks like he hasn't been there in weeks - and he hasn't returned to the boxing ring where he works. So, anyone not involved in a Major Crimes case - i.e. murder or abduction - is to make this search your top priority. I want you out there talking to everyone in Keane's and Barrett's neighborhoods. Bums, prostitutes, pushers, newspaper vendors, hot dog vendors, store clerks, little old ladies and neighborhood busybodies - not just people who live on the same block."

He paused to let everyone pore over the photographs. "Barrett is a subcontractor and a licensed freelance electrician. He also has a history of arson. You've seen what he can do - expect that and more. I'll be talking to his recent employers, but I also want his apartment under constant surveillance. Same goes for the boxing ring. And I want someone to continue to stand guard outside Vincent Perry's and Neil Coates' hospital rooms. Your Lieutenants will assign those posts. Bottom line: I want Barrett. Get him by midnight and there's a commendation in it for you." The officers seemed to perk up at this. "I suggest you get going."

The officers dispersed, leaving the precinct with photos in hand. All except one. A fresh-faced young officer with light brown hair hung back and approached Noah once the others had gone.

"Detective Harkham," the young officer said, "I'm John Reynolds...Officer Reynolds," he amended. He held out his hand and Noah shook it, unsure what to expect from this kid. "Sir, I was just wondering, does this mean you've come back to the force? I mean, everyone is talking, sir, speculating -"

"Yes, I heard. And saw," Noah said. "Listen - Reynolds, is it? Do me a favor."

The rookie brightened. "Of course, sir."

"Try not to forget that I can still see and hear, even if only on one side. And I'm not stupid, or any slower or less sharp than I was on the job because of this," he said, gesturing to the left side of his face.

"Make sure you and everyone keeps that in mind, all right? Because, while no, I am not back on the force, I will be assisting in this investigation, so I will be around. Any talking, any speculating - any laughing - they want to do is fine by me, but if they're going to do it behind their hands right in front of me, they're going to have to be prepared to say it to my face."

He kept his expression as neutral as possible and didn't once raise his voice, but the anger coursing through his body was making the heat rise in him. "Do you understand, Officer?"

Reynolds looked mortified, and as hurt as if Noah had struck him. "Y-yes, sir. I wasn't - I'm sorry, sir."

Noah took a second to calm down. "Don't be. You seem like a decent guy. Just - just get out there and find this guy."

"Yes, sir," Reynolds nodded. "I'll do my best." He started to walk away, but turned back. "Seven years ago you worked a case in James Park. A little girl, eleven years old, was killed by a hit-and-run. You and Detective Franks caught the guy and you came to personally tell the family that, even though it wouldn't change the nightmare they were going through, they could at least know this guy would never hurt anyone else like that. You felt their grief, and they knew it."

This time it was Noah who felt like he'd been struck. "I remember her." He flicked a glance at Frankie. "Tasha Bailey. She had coal black hair, all in curls, big brown eyes and a red raincoat." He grimaced. "The rain made it hard to get the evidence."

Reynolds nodded. "Tasha was my little sister's best friend. She was at our house at least every weekend, if not more. I'd always wanted to be a cop, but after that, I wanted to be you." He paused a moment. "Not all of us are laughing, Detective. You try to keep that in mind, all right?" He turned and walked away, leaving Noah staring after him, feeling like a jerk.

He felt Frankie watching him, but couldn't look him in the eye. Without a word, he left, pushing through the precinct's front door to stand on the stoop. Guilt for lashing out at Reynolds and the unexpected reminder of that gut-punch of a case left him feeling... brittle. He needed to do something, needed to be of use.

Frankie joined him a moment later. "I want to talk to old Mister Keane," Noah told him. "Today. If he was lucid enough to tell Cox and Adelmo his name, maybe we'll get lucky and he can tell us where to find his son. Or the name of someone who can."

CHAPTER THIRTY-NINE

───

ROBIN HEADED BACK DOWNSTAIRS toward the hospital's main lobby. She'd spent the morning with Neil, staying with him until he'd fallen asleep. She turned a corner and was surprised to see Frankie and Noah Harkham speaking to Officers Cox and Adelmo. The first thing she noticed was the butterfly closure on Noah's cheek and his split lip. Apparently, it didn't go very well with Bobby Avalon.

Noah saw her and slipped past the others to come join her, stopping short with a slight flinch to let a nurse who'd come up unseen on his left side pass by. "Hey, Shots," he said, once he was close by.

"Hey," she said. She gestured toward his face. "I take it you talked to Avalon?"

"Yeah," he gave a short, rueful laugh. "How did you know? That he would know anything about Barrett?"

"Frankie told you what led us to him in the first place, right?"

He nodded. "The Colt."

"Yeah. I found out the gun used to shoot Vincent Perry is the same one used in a series of robberies right around the time of the Brookview fire. The same kind of gun Bobby Avalon said was stolen the day before the fire. I just figured that if Tony Barrett took the gun - stole it or borrowed it, what have you - it meant he knew Bobby Avalon fairly well. I thought maybe he'd go to Avalon for help now, since most of these low-life types tend to sink into the same pits together, don't they?"

183

Noah nodded with a half grin. "Turns out you were right. We've got a lead on how to track Barrett down out of it. Along with," he added with a smile and gesture toward the cuts on his face.

"Great," she replied with an excited smile. "Well, not the punch in the face part, obviously. So... what are you guys doing down here, then?"

"Avalon's cut man treated Barrett, then called in someone else when he saw the injury was too much for him to handle himself. We went looking for the cut man, Sam Keane, but found his neglected, malnourished father living in filth instead."

"That's awful," she said.

He nodded. "Poor old man's got dementia, but we're hoping once he's hydrated and fed, he might be able to tell us how to find his son."

Behind him, a nurse called out to an elderly man who had just exited a room. "No, no, darling, you need to go back in your room. They're not done getting you fixed up."

Noah turned. "That's the father," he said, his brow crinkling with concern.

Mister Keane was mumbling something they couldn't hear to the nurse, but, when he turned and saw Robin, he stopped speaking and a big smile brightened his face. "There you are," he said as he approached. "I thought I'd lost you."

She looked from Noah to the nurse. They both shrugged. "Uh, no, I'm not lost," she told him with a smile. "I'm right here." She took his arm and gently steered him back towards his room. "Why don't we go and sit down?"

"That sounds lovely," he said, patting her hand.

She led the old Mister Keane back to his room and settled next to him on the bed. He continued to pat her hand and smiled wistfully at her, but didn't say anything else for a few minutes.

Noah and Frankie came in just a moment later. Frankie knelt in front of him. "Mister Keane, I'm Detective Franks, Riverdale PD. Can you tell me where to find your son, Samuel?"

"My name is Samuel."

Frankie glanced at Robin, then said, "Right, but your son, his name is Samuel, too, isn't that right?"

"My son..." Mister Keane's mind seemed to wander. "I've got it all wrote down, remember?" His voice was tremulous. "We wrote it all down. I remember, Sammy."

Robin furrowed her brow and shot Frankie an inquiring look. "There was a list on the kitchen counter of things for him to remember to do each day," he supplied. "Things like brush his teeth, use the toilet, when and what to eat...As if that could take the place of someone looking after him." The muscle of his jaw twitched and his expression had hardened.

"You've got to be kidding," she said, feeling protective of this elderly man she just met.

"I wish we were," Noah said.

A nurse came in to take his blood pressure and bring him some food. He elected to sit in the plush armchair next to the bed while he ate, but Robin remained seated on the edge of the bed. "Let me try something," she said, getting off the bed and kneeling in front of the old man. She put her hand on his frail arm. "Samuel," she said. "Samuel, it's me."

He seemed to freeze, then slowly turned his rheumy blue eyes toward her. "Hannah?"

She smiled. "Samuel, this is very important - do you know where Sammy is?"

"Sammy?" He's out playin' ball in the sandlot."

"No, Samuel - where is he now? Sammy's all grown up now. He was at your apartment the other day. Do you remember?"

"My...apartment..." his gaze turned far away and she feared they had lost his attention again. But a tear broke free of his lashes as he nodded to himself. "My apartment, after I lost my Hannah." He looked at her again. "You're not my Hannah."

His expression broke her heart. "No, Samuel, I'm sorry, I'm not. But it is really important that we find your son, Sammy. We need his help. Can you tell me how to find him?"

"You must be Robbie's girl, then. Amelia...the animal doctor?" He smiled and leaned forward. "I'm your grandpa Sam - what do you think of that, eh?"

Robin smiled. "I think you make a wonderful grandpa."

He smiled back at her, patting her hand, and began humming tunelessly. She slipped her hand from under his and stood to face Noah and Frankie with a shrug. "Worth a shot," she said.

"It might have helped a lot, if what he says is true," Noah said.

"Yeah, if so, he has a granddaughter who's a veterinarian," Frankie agreed. "She might have been the woman Stitch called. I'll make some calls, try to find Robert Keane, or, on the off chance she's unmarried, a vet named Amelia Keane." He nodded to Robin. "Thanks, Shots."

She smiled. "You bet."

Frankie clapped Noah's shoulder on his way out. "I'll be in touch."

"Yep," Noah said by way of farewell.

Robin noticed Samuel had dozed off and so whispered to Noah, "Visiting hours are over for now, but I bet they would let you look in on Neil, if you want to."

"Yeah." He nodded. "Yeah, I think I need to see him."

They navigated through the corridor back to the main lobby and took the elevator to the second floor. The nurse at the ICU station recognized them from before and told them Neil was sleeping, but they could look in on him through the glass as long as they didn't wake him. She also prepared Noah for all the machines and monitors he'd see his cousin hooked up to.

"It looks worse than it is," Robin assured him. "And they say it's only temporary until the swelling goes down."

The nurse nodded and, when Noah asked, said she expected Neil to be transferred out of the ICU and into a regular room once his blood pressure stabilized. "No more than a few days from now, I should think," she said. "And barring any secondary infections or other complications, he should be fine soon after that."

"Thank you," Noah said, sounding relieved. The nurse smiled and led them to the window overlooking Neil's room, then let them have some time to themselves.

"How can he sleep with all that noise?" Noah asked. They could hear the various beeps and hisses of all the different machines through the glass.

"He's still exhausted. He lost a lot of blood." She shivered at the thought of how close they came to losing him.

Noah looked away from his cousin and back to her. He looked as if he were going to say something, but changed his mind and turned his attention back to Neil. She tilted her head, trying to get him to look at her again. "What were you going to say?"

His eyes slid toward her, then he faced her. "It's just... Neil mentioned once a while back the two of you have been discussing your faith. He said that - we were told growing up that God is real and Jesus died in our place, okay? But he said it had never really felt real to him until recently, but I don't know if..."

He shifted his stance and looked down at the floor. "I was just thinking, if you are right - I mean, he *died* yesterday. Twice. What if he had - if they hadn't been able to-" He shook his head.

"Hey," she said, touching his arm, "he didn't and they were. But even if he had died, permanently, yesterday or whenever he does - which I'm sure won't be for a very long time - just know you don't need to worry about him, as far as eternity goes."

She eyed him for a moment. "But maybe it isn't just him you're worried about?"

He looked up sharply, then, slowly, his expression softened. "It's not like I don't know God's there... I do, it's just..." He sighed. "How can He ever forgive me when I'm not sure I can forgive Him?"

She brought her hand up, not quite touching his scars. "For this?"

He turned away, back to the glass and she thought for a minute he wouldn't answer. But then he quietly said, "For a lot of things."

"He'll always forgive you, Noah, if you ask. God loves you. Always. I hope you can believe that." She offered up another prayer of thanks that Neil was alive, and added a request for Noah's angry heart and soul to be healed, too. Then, she steeled herself to say something she'd been meaning to tell Noah for months. "And I hope you can forgive me."

He frowned at her. "What are you talking about?"

She took a breath and plunged into what she had often practiced saying to him. "It's no excuse, but your trial was one of the first and certainly the biggest in which I had testified here in Riverdale. The biggest case I'd ever testified in, really," she added, looking away from his face and focusing on his shoes instead. They were black and clean, though they had some miles on them. Probably ones he'd worn on the job.

"I was nervous and Avalon's lawyer...he just chewed me up and spit me out," she said. "I should've been more confident, shouldn't have let him rattle me so much. It was unprofessional, I know. The evidence was there, I just didn't make it speak loudly enough."

Avalon's lawyer, Andrew Lester - AKA The Weasel - had been able to get him off on the attempted murder and aggravated assault of a police officer charges. He'd only been indicted on the charges of illegal discharge of a weapon inside city limits and reckless endangerment. He was sentenced to sixteen months and a $2,500 fine, plus one year probation. For half blinding and half deafening a cop and ending his career.

He'd gotten out early for good behavior.

Robin had commended Noah, calling him a hero for taking down the suspect without firing his weapon, which would have endangered Officer Cox, who was standing in the line of fire. The Weasel had jumped all over her use of the word hero, saying Noah had been nothing but a glory-hound, a hotshot out to get all the credit for taking the suspect down himself, but ended up getting himself wounded instead. He insisted Avalon had been in the process of surrendering his weapon to Officer Adelmo and it was only the force of being thrown to the ground that caused the gun to fire. That, essentially, Noah had done it to himself.

The jury was won over. Her arguments that the gun would not have fired if Avalon's finger had not been on the trigger and that, if he had fired it from where he was standing, the bullet would have hit Adelmo in the chest - a fatal shot at that close range - all seemed to be summarily dismissed in their minds once The Weasel finished his closing arguments.

She shrugged and forced herself to face him again. "I let you down. I'm sorry."

"I never blamed you," he said, looking surprised at her confession. "Avalon was a bit of a celebrity a few years back, and some of the jury remembered that. And his lawyer is a slippery little charmer. They just swallowed the whole package as he sold it to them. You saw it, he had them convinced my career wasn't over, just different. I was alive, and at that time, they didn't know if my injuries would be permanent, blah, blah, blah." He made a dismissive gesture. "It wasn't your fault. It's just how it went."

"But if I hadn't been so nervous, if I hadn't acted like a stupid, green rookie, I could have-"

"It wasn't your fault. Okay? It happened and it's over. If you're looking for forgiveness, I won't give it, because there's nothing to forgive."

She held his gaze for a long moment, wrestling with his lack of reproach. Then, with a deep breath, she nodded. "Thank you," she said, "but it still sucks it turned out that way."

"Yeah, it does," he smirked. After looking at Neil one more time, he said, "Come on, I owe you a shot of whiskey for the whole Avalon thing."

She grimaced. "Yeah, I'll pass. But I'll let you buy me a Coke from the vending machine."

He laughed. "Deal."

CHAPTER FORTY

———

FRANKIE AND THE ADA, Gerald Warner, stared down Bobby Avalon and his lawyer across the table. Gerald steepled his fingers and said, "Mr. Avalon, you are willing to aid in the capture and indictment of a murderer, are you not? Are you willing to testify Samuel Keane provided medical treatment to Tony Barrett in your facility?"

Avalon's lawyer, Andrew "The Weasel" Lester, passed a cool eye over them both. "My client has been advised not to answer any questions until we have an acceptable deal on the table. He is only willing to testify if his cooperation is richly rewarded."

Frankie and Warner exchanged a look. "In that case," Warner said, "we are willing to forget about the accessory after the fact charge and settle for the lesser charge of aiding and abetting a fugitive."

"Time?"

"Three years with an additional two years' probation and a twenty thousand dollar fine. Plus, your client will be subject to random audits of his company accounts."

Avalon threw a worried look at The Weasel. "That's ridiculous!" Lester said. "My client's company had nothing to do with this."

Warner's expression soured. "He allowed a man with no medical training to provide treatment and medication to a murder suspect in his place of business. Mister Avalon has also admitted that this individual is paid under the table and is not on the company's official payroll. All entities involved in the commission of a crime are subject to penalty in recompense for the crime."

There was a glint in his eye as he continued. "And, as you know, Mister Lester, a company is a legally liable entity. The IRS has graciously agreed to a schedule of random audits instead of seizing his assets and a federal indictment of their own, but only if he agrees to this deal." He turned his attention to Avalon. "We can unleash the IRS on you if you'd rather, Mister Avalon."

"He's already provided the name of the cut man who treated Barrett," Frankie said to Warner, as if it were a side conversation just between them, but kept his voice loud enough for Avalon to hear, "which he did without expectation of any reward. We have enough to charge Barrett once he's apprehended without Avalon's testimony. If he doesn't want the deal, I still have him on the hook for all of it. It makes no difference to my case whether he testifies or rots in prison for life." His patience for these maneuverings was running out. If Avalon didn't take the bait, he was set to make good on this threat.

After taking old Mister Keane to the hospital last night, Frankie had gone home exhausted and hoping to sleep like a log. But instead, he had lain awake thinking of places to look for Barrett and playing out different scenarios in which he'd be captured. This morning, he'd gotten to the precinct before seven, called the meeting with Noah and the uniform officers and then sent the cops out with pictures of Barrett and Keane. All he wanted now was to get this dog and pony show over with so he could spend some quality time with a pillow.

"That carries a fifteen year sentence, Mister Avalon," Warner informed the boxer.

Avalon looked back and forth between Warner and The Weasel. "I want to take it, Lester," he said, desperation choking his voice.

The Weasel silenced him with a curt gesture. Then he smiled in that sickening-sweet way he did when addressing a jury. "Nonsense, Mister Avalon; don't give up so easily. The negotiations have just begun."

"No, Mister Lester, they haven't," Warner cut in. "The DA's office is not willing to haggle on terms in this case. The charges awaiting Anthony Barrett are of a very serious nature and the fact your client played a critical role in allowing him to evade capture does not engender any sympathy or generosity in the judicial community." He held The Weasel's cool glare.

A moment passed, and when The Weasel did not answer, Warner turned to Frankie. "It's obvious we're wasting our time here, Detective. I'm sure it could be put to much better use by pursuing the information Mister Avalon so generously gave you."

He and Frankie both stood, gathering up the case file and their notebooks. "Wait! You'd have nothin' without me," Avalon said, his voice rising. "That's gotta get me somethin'! We had a deal!"

"Actually, Bobby," Frankie said, leaning on his fists across the table to look Avalon in the eye, "I have you on tape saying, and I quote, 'that much is free. If you want more, you get me a lawyer and a deal,' end quote. So you see, we don't owe you a damn thing."

"They're bluffing, Bobby," The Weasel affirmed. "They're trying to bully you into playing on their terms." He shuffled his papers self-importantly and stood to face them. "If they had a leg to stand on in this case, and if they had any hope of getting your accessory charge to stick, they wouldn't be trying to scare you into talking. Go ahead, gentlemen, we're calling your bluff. Even if you did somehow go to trial, Bobby, there's not a jury in the world that would buy their 'evidence' once I'm through chatting with them."

He smiled his best oily smile at Frankie and Warner. "After all, if you couldn't get him more than a slap on the wrist for blinding and deafening a cop, well, then..." He winked at Frankie, letting the gesture and his smile finish the thought.

"Come on, Mister Avalon," The Weasel said, assisting his client to his feet. "Have a wonderful day, gentlemen," he added, escorting his shackled client out of the interrogation room.

"Right," Frankie said with a sigh, too tired to let The Weasel's remarks about Noah rile him, "I guess now we inform the DA we're charging him with accessory after the fact on top of the rest. The IRS will get to sink their teeth into him, too, the stupid clod." He extended his hand, which Warner shook. "Thanks, Gerald."

"Not a problem. How goes the search for Barrett and Keane, anyway?"

"I'm hoping to have them both in custody by the weekend and to hand you the case on Monday."

"Sounds good," he said with a grin. He started toward the door, but stopped and leaned in to whisper, "Remember to get some sleep once this is over, okay?"

Frankie scoffed. "Is it that obvious?"

Warner merely tilted his head with a half-smile and walked out the door.

FRANKIE GOT BACK TO his desk a few minutes later. He'd left the list of contractors and clients Barrett had worked with in the past there and settled in to start calling them. Before he could, however, Ziehring came in, practically stomping his way from the door.

As he passed Frankie's desk, he commanded, "My office."

"Here it comes," Frankie muttered to himself, getting up and following his boss.

He shut the door and turned to see Ziehring with one hand on his hip and the other rubbing his temples. "Do you want to tell me what the hell you were thinking?"

"Sir?"

He gave him a look. "Don't play stupid, Franks. I had to hear it from a bunch of uniforms that Noah Harkham is assisting with the biggest case this squad has seen all year. Tell me, Detective, just *exactly* how is he assisting in this case?"

"He's helped in getting information that has led to new leads. He's been very helpful."

"Oh, well I'm so glad you've enjoyed having him around," Ziehring said, "because it may very well end up costing us this case. Do you have any idea what that weasel Andrew Lester will do with the knowledge that Noah was anywhere near his client without being authorized by the department?"

Frankie swallowed hard. This was exactly what he was afraid would happen, and yet he had gone in headlong anyway. "Sir, Noah did nothing out of line. All he did was ask Bobby Avalon to give me the information I needed. Avalon gave it." He looked his boss in the eye.

"He needed to be involved, sir. One way or another." He spread his hands. "This has been nothing more than a routine civilian ride-along. Except Noah's not exactly a civilian."

Ziehring let out a breath. "No, he isn't, is he? He's not exactly a civilian and he's not exactly a cop. That's just the beginning of the problem," he ran a hand down his tie, thinking, "but maybe it can be the beginning of the solution."

Frankie furrowed his brow. "Sir?"

Ziehring walked around to stand behind his desk and leveled a stern look at him. "*Consultant* Harkham is not to have any more access to witnesses or suspects outside this precinct. Nor is he to be anywhere near a gun. He is to let you do all the talking if you do bring in a suspect or witness, or at least don't let him interrogate them directly. Do you understand, Detective?"

He grinned. "Yes, sir."

Ziehring sat with a weary sigh and reached for the phone. "I've got to get him on the books before Lester has a chance to rip us apart with this," he grumbled. He flicked his gaze back up. "Are you still here?"

"No, sir," Frankie said, suppressing another smile, and left the room.

———————————

WHEN HE GOT BACK TO his desk, Noah was sitting in his chair. He gave him a look, but Noah ignored it and asked, "How mad is he?"

Frankie scoffed and grabbed his mug off the desk. "Coffee?"

Noah pulled a face, but nodded. "Sure."

Frankie went to the break room in the corner. He rinsed his mug before filling it with coffee. He grabbed a second mug out of the cabinet and filled it for Noah. He snagged a handful of sugar packets and a couple of swizzle sticks and went back to his desk. Noah gave up the chair and carefully balanced himself and his coffee mug on the edge of the desk instead. He dumped four packets of sugar into his brew, giving it a thorough stirring with the swizzle stick. Noah drank his coffee black.

"You look as tired as I feel," Noah commented.

He grunted. "Can't sleep with this one."

Noah nodded. "Yeah."

Frankie's computer beeped, and he opened the window for the records search he had been running. "Looks like we got lucky: the search pulled up a veterinary license for Amelia Keane. Says she works at a small vet clinic down by the riverfront. Her current address is..." he ran a DMV search. "2233 Westwood Avenue, apartment B19." He looked at Noah. "Even if she isn't the one Stitch called, she might know some of the people her uncle keeps company with. Either way, maybe we can convince her to help us find him." He stood and grabbed his suit jacket and keys.

"We?" Noah asked, also rising.

"Just remember, as a consultant, you are here to advise only. I get to do all the talking. Okay?"

"Copy that, boss," Noah said with a smile. "Lead the way."

CHAPTER FORTY-ONE

SEVERAL MINUTES LATER, they stood at the door of Amelia Keane's apartment. It was just after nine o'clock on Saturday morning and when the doctor answered the door, she was still dressed for bed. Frankie had held up his badge so she could see it through the peep hole, and yet she still only opened the door as far as the chain allowed. "Yes?" Her voice was guarded.

"Dr. Amelia Keane?"

She looked pale. "Yes."

"I'm Detective Franks, Riverdale PD. This is Noah Harkham, a consultant for the department. We need to ask you a few questions, may we come in?"

She dropped her gaze before answering. "Of course. Just a moment." She shut the door and they could hear the chain being unlatched. There was a slight pause before the door opened again. She cinched her fuzzy lavender bathrobe tighter around her thin body and smoothed her black hair as she stepped aside to let them in. "Please, have a seat," she invited and seated herself on an overstuffed brown suede chair.

The apartment was neat, for the most part, but there were books, magazines and cups in random places, like she hadn't tidied up for a day or two. A glance toward the kitchen to their left revealed a sink full of dishes. But the brown suede couch they sat on was clean and comfortable.

Amelia's gaze darted back and forth between them. She held herself ram-rod stiff, her hands tightly folded together. She was nervous; but was it just the nervousness of someone not used to having cops in her home or did she know why they were here?

"So what is all this about, Detectives?"

"We're in the process of investigating a case and the name Sam Keane has come up. He's your uncle, isn't that right?"

"I have an uncle and a grandfather by that name, yes. Has something happened to him?"

"We're hoping he can give us some information. But if you're worried about his safety, we could check on him for you, if you could tell us where we might find him."

She hesitated. "He's done something wrong, hasn't he?"

Frankie dipped his head. "Again, ma'am, we just need to find him. We went to the address on his license and we found a building that ought to be condemned and your grandfather living in squalor. Your uncle was nowhere to be found."

Now her concern seemed genuine. "Is Grandpa all right? Where is he?"

"He's fine, Dr. Keane," Noah interjected. "He was a little malnourished and seemed a little confused, but he's being looked after."

"And just as soon as you let us know where to find your uncle, we can take you to see your grandfather."

Her eyes hardened. "Oh, I see. You won't tell me where he is unless I tell you where Uncle Sammy is. You aren't concerned about his well-being at all; you just want to pin something on him. Isn't that right?" she asked, mocking Frankie's earlier question.

"We just need some information," Noah said, making a placating gesture. "Whatever your uncle may or may not have done pales in comparison to what the man we're looking for has done. Where-"

"Where is he, Dr. Keane?" Frankie cut in before Noah could question her.

She turned from Frankie to Noah, looking at him directly for the first time, and froze. Her eyes were fixed on the scars he bore and the new wounds to go with them. "Noah Harkham," she whispered. "My uncle works for Bobby Avalon, which I'm guessing you already know."

She sighed in resignation. "My uncle is not a good man, but years ago he did something for me I thought I could never repay. I was wrong." She faced Frankie again. "I don't know where my uncle is, but I can give you Tony Barrett. That is who you're looking for, isn't it?"

"I'm listening," he said, stunned.

She chafed her palms together. "This is going to cost me my license, if not my life. But I can't do this anymore. Maybe now I can finally be free of him." She let out a shaky breath. "I've lost count of how many bullets I've removed, how many knife wounds I've sewn up, how many scumbags I've put back together for him. All because he threatened to make the phone call that would cost me everything." She gave a bitter, humorless laugh. "Ah, irony."

She reached for a small notepad and pen on the end table next to her. She scribbled something on it, tore the page off and handed it to Frankie. "I left him there, yesterday afternoon. He lost quite a bit of blood, and I didn't have any to transfuse. He's weak; he'll still be there, or not very far, for at least another day."

"Thank you, Amelia," Noah told her with feeling.

Frankie nodded to her. "We'll need you to come to the station, give a formal statement."

"Yes, I suppose you do." She wiped her hands on her robe. "For the record, I had all but decided to come forward today anyway. I've already drafted my letter of resignation." She took a moment, then stood. "If you'll give me just a minute to get dressed, I'll be ready."

They both stood. "Of course," Frankie said.

She looked at each of them in turn before heading down the hall between the living room and kitchen. A moment later, they heard her shut her bedroom door. They sat back down to wait.

"What do you think?" Noah asked.

"You mean, am I surprised she's turned on her uncle and willing to lose everything to help us out?" He thought it over. "I don't know, she seemed sincere. Like she was tired of it all. But I'm not sure she's thought this all through. Yes, she knows she's going to lose her practice, but she's also gonna face charges." He read the address on the paper she had given him. Something about it felt familiar...

"Yeah, but, given that she just handed us Barrett on a silver platter, I think Gerald might be able to get her a good deal."

Frankie stood. "Yeah, probably." He headed down the hall a little way.

"What is it?" Noah asked, following a few steps behind.

"She's taking a long time, right?"

"Some women take a while to get dressed," Noah said, but Frankie saw his hand stray to where he used to carry his gun.

"You think she's running?" Frankie asked.

Before Noah could answer, they heard a dull clatter. They froze, listening. Then there was a loud thump as something hit the wall. Frankie drew his gun and rushed to the door. He shouldered it open and ducked inside after checking his entry.

Amelia Keane stood over the limp form of Sammy "The Stitch" Keane, her robe, nightgown and hair in disarray. There were tears in her eyes and a broken alarm clock in her hand. Frankie put his gun away and went to her.

"Are you all right? What happened?" he asked, steering her to sit on the edge of the bed.

Noah knelt and checked Sammy for a pulse. "He's alive," he announced, pulling out his phone and calling for an ambulance.

Amelia was trembling. "I don't know how he got in here." She glanced at the closed window with a sniff. "I tried to get him to leave but he said he couldn't let me talk. He was going to kill me."

"We were just outside. Why didn't you call out?" Frankie asked, incredulous.

She looked at him, her tear-stained face blank. "He's family."

CHAPTER FORTY-TWO

———

IT WAS THE YOUNG COP, Reynolds, and another one who Noah wasn't familiar with named Ryzowski who responded to the call along with the ambulance. Frankie gave them orders to take Amelia back to the station, make her comfortable and take her statement. The paramedics, meanwhile, loaded Sammy Keane up in the ambulance to take him to County General.

Reynolds overheard Frankie telling the paramedics he was going to have officers meet them at the ER to stand guard on Keane and volunteered for the job himself. "It only takes one of us to drive a witness back to the station. I can stay with this guy every step of the way. It makes more sense than waiting for someone else."

"Right, do it," Frankie told him. "Get on the rig." Reynolds nodded and started up into the ambulance. Frankie grabbed his arm, stalling him. "You let him out of your sight for a second and you'll be on desk duty for a year."

"Yes, sir." Reynolds climbed into the ambulance. Frankie shut the doors and banged on them twice to signal the driver to move out.

Officer Ryzowski drove her cruiser past them, Amelia Keane in the back. Noah nodded to her, receiving a troubled smile in return. "She's going to feel guilty for a while," he said to Frankie, "but I think she's also relieved. She's free of him now, at least."

"Yeah," Frankie agreed. He pulled the slip of paper she had given him from his pocket and lifted his eyebrows at Noah. "You ready for this?"

"I am," he replied.

Frankie nodded and lifted his radio. "2914 to Dispatch."

"Copy, 2914. Go ahead."

Noah flashed a smile. "Joyce. Just like old times. That's a good sign."

"You getting superstitious on me, partner?" Frankie asked with a grin. Into his radio he then said, "Dispatch, I have a 10-20 on our suspect, Joseph Anthony Barrett." He looked at the paper and paused, releasing the transmit button on his radio. "Hark," he said. His expression was strange.

"What is it?"

The radio crackled. "2914, say again your last. Transmission incomplete, over."

"This address, it's Simon Turner's building."

Noah frowned. "The one he burned down?"

"No, look - his building, where he lives. Or did, before he was arrested. It's Turner Heights."

"2914, come in, over."

"What's Simon Turner got to do with this?" Noah asked.

"I don't know, but we're about to find out." He punched down the radio button. "Dispatch, I need all available units 10-40 to 2009 Lake Drive, the Turner Heights building." He and Noah rushed to Frankie's car. "I am en route, ETA fifteen minutes, over." He started the Chrysler and the engine roared to life.

"Copy, 2914. Shall I have rescue units on standby?"

"Affirmative. Fire and medical - I don't know what to expect from this guy. Out." Frankie lurched the car into traffic, virtually flying through the streets. He switched on his lights and siren to help clear the way.

"Strap in," he commanded unnecessarily, since Noah already was fastening his belt in anticipation of how fast Frankie would have to drive to get across town in fifteen minutes.

When they were partners, Noah almost always let Frankie do all the driving. Most people in this city drive like idiots, and, as much as his masculine pride didn't want him to admit it, Frankie was a better driver. He had reflexes like a race car driver and tended to drive like one, too. Noah was long since used to this and was barely phased by the tiny openings he slipped the car through or the quick lane changes and short braking distances he allowed.

Several times Frankie had to put on the lights and siren just to make headway, but as they drew closer to their destination, he complied with his own 10-40 request, driving without lights or siren so as not to tip off Barrett they were coming. His concentration was fixed on the traffic around them, but Noah's was fixed on the knot of twisting electric energy squirming in his gut.

It was a familiar sensation, and one he thought never to experience again - the thrill of the hunt, some might say. But this time was different: more urgent, more personal. This time they hunted the man who had almost killed Neil; who had intended to kill him instead. And this guy was close to Bobby Avalon.

Yes, this time it was very personal.

His fingers itched for action and he wiped his hands on his thighs to still them. "There it is," Frankie's voice broke through his thoughts. He pointed to the imposing visage of Turner Heights as it loomed into view. He slowed, nodding to the several other units parked as discreetly as possible along the block. None had their lights or sirens on, but all those cop cars in one place would be hard to miss.

Noah leaned forward in anticipation. "All he has to do is look out a window," he grumbled, jouncing his left leg.

"Then we move fast. Even if he does bolt, there's no place that doesn't have a cop watching it." He parked and they both got out. "He's as good as ours, Hark. Don't worry about it."

As they crossed the street, some of the other officers joined them. "Seal off the roads around the building, one block radius," Frankie instructed them. "Break out the barricades and reroute traffic. This guy is fond of fire, so I don't want to take any chances. I want someone at every corner and each exit. Where's Branson?" He stopped on the sidewalk before the building and looked for the officer.

"Here, sir," he said from the back of the group.

"I want you on the east fire escape. It services the apartment Barrett's holed up in. Cox and Adelmo -"

"Behind you, Frankie," Adelmo said.

He turned to them. "You two are going in with me. I want another team coming in behind us to clear the neighboring apartments - on the floor of the apartment and the ones above and below it, just in case." He selected six officers and then said, "Everyone else, get on crowd control. We need to keep this quiet and calm. That's it, get into position." The officers snapped into action.

As Frankie headed toward the entrance with Cox and Adelmo, Noah moved to follow. Frankie stopped him. "Whoa, I can't let you in there."

"What? No, Frankie, you've got to-"

"No way. I'm not putting you in harm's way - or jeopardizing this operation. We do this my way this time, all right?" Frankie stared him down until he nodded. "But if you were to happen to be in the alley off the fire escape, you could potentially help Stiles spot Barrett if he gets past Branson and heads toward the subway."

Noah choked back his initial anger and saw not only that Frankie was right, but was doing the one thing he could to keep Noah part of this. "Got it." Stiles was a good cop, and though they weren't exactly friends, they had worked well together in the past.

The sound of a vehicle approaching redirected their attention. It was Ziehring. He exited the car and caught sight of Frankie. "Go on, Franks," he said with a dismissive wave of his hand. "I'm only here to help coordinate, this is your bust."

Frankie nodded and he and Noah headed into position. Noah found Stiles and followed him to the east alley. Amelia said she'd left Barrett in an apartment on the fifth floor. He counted up and over to the window Barrett would have to use and noticed Branson making his way up the metal steps as quietly as possible. Even from here, Noah could see the officer appeared nervous and wondered if this was his first big take down.

"Just so you know," Stiles told him, "I think you're insane for getting yourself involved in this, Harkham." He then grinned. "It's good to have you back, you ballsy son." He clapped Noah on the shoulder with a chuckle.

"Uh, thanks, Stiles."

"But if you get me shot," he continued, his face now serious, "I'm going to kill you."

"Got it."

Several agonizingly long minutes dragged by with no sign what was happening inside the building. Then Stiles' radio emitted a short burst of static, followed by an officer's voice stating, "We're getting quite an audience building up at the north barricade. Request extra units, if available. Over."

This request was followed by a terse reply, "All units posted elsewhere." It was Ziehring. Noah detected the strain in his former captain's voice, which was understandable given that the department was going after this guy with everything they've got. He was no doubt feeling the pressure to bring this to a satisfactory end as quickly as possible. "Advise bystanders of potential personal injury and strongly suggest they vacate the premises. Out."

The radio fuzzed again. "All units standby." It was Frankie this time. "The suspect does not appear to be on the premises... Confirmed: suspect is in the wind," he announced, frustration and anger coloring his report.

"What the hell?" Stiles turned to frown at Harkham. "He knew we were coming, didn't he?"

"You're asking me?" Noah countered. Growling a curse under his breath, he kicked over a nearby trashcan.

"Hey, relax," Stiles said. "He can't have gotten far, right? He isn't strong enough. It's only a matter of time."

Noah shrugged and started to reply, but commotion from the north barricade distracted him. "Now what?" He stalked over to check it out.

The crowd gathered there to rubberneck had erupted into shouts and fits of shoving. He grabbed the arm of the nearest officer manning the barricade and shouted over the crowd. "You gotta keep these people under control! What's going on?"

The officer tried to respond, but his voice was drowned out by the shouting of the others. Noah gestured to him to wait and turned to the people. "Everyone shut the hell up!"

"Hey, screw you, pig!" someone replied. "You can't keep us from going home!" Other people took up variations of these sentiments.

"Calm down! If you do not calm down now, you will be escorted from the area and detained at the station."

"You can't do that!" several people said.

Noah leaned in toward the officer's right ear. "Tell Ziehring you may end up needing some riot gear over here."

The officer said something, but movement at the mouth of the next side street up caught Noah's attention. It was a man of slight build shuffling around the corner toward the building, his arm in a sling. He looked up at the sound of the crowd shouting.

Their eyes met. Noah's breath caught in his throat. "It's him," he said. He turned his head a fraction, keeping Barrett in sight, and shouted over his shoulder to the officer. "That's him - call it in."

Tony Barrett fumbled in his pocket with his good hand and withdrew a slim object. Noah reached for the gun he belatedly realized he didn't have -

A concussive blast thundered from the building, raining shattered glass from Barrett's apartment onto those in the street and alley below. Noah instinctively ducked and covered his head with his hands, but then peered through the dust back to where Barrett had been.

He was gone.

Frankie.

Noah shot to his feet amid a rush of people - officers and panicked bystanders alike. He hesitated, looking from where Barrett had stood back to the building in which his best friend might be injured. Stiles stumbled out of the alley, his face streaming blood from half a dozen or more cuts and contusions. He wiped his eyes clear with one hand and approached Noah with his other hand outstretched.

Noah wavered a split second longer. "Shit!" he spat, going into the alley to grab Stiles' arm. "Stiles? You okay?" The officer nodded. "Where's Frankie and the others?" Stiles gaped at him, still dazed. "Did they make it out?"

"I... I dunno... All I saw was glass and concrete."

Noah looked past him to the end of the alley, where he could see a knot of officers and rescue personnel rushing toward the building's front entrance. Neither Frankie nor anyone who'd gone in with him were among them. Noah bit back another curse and snatched Stiles' radio and gun.

"What are you -?"

"Barrett was here. Down the street. He triggered the explosion. Tell Ziehring he's either headed east or south," he told him, walking backwards toward the street. "Get some uniforms to start canvassing. And find Frankie and the others."

He turned and ran toward the side street Barrett had first emerged from, ignoring Stiles' protests. He had to push his way through a knot of fleeing bystanders twice before turning the corner. A knocked over bicycle still had its wheel spinning, evidence Barrett wasn't too far ahead of him, despite his hesitation. No doubt his injury and blood loss was making him slow and clumsy, much to Noah's advantage.

He raced to the opposite end of the block and ducked his head around the corner to the left, then leaned out to peer to the right. He had to lean further than was safe to get a clear line of sight with his right eye instead of his useless left one. He hoped Barrett didn't still have his gun, as he was making a nice, clear target of himself...

There was no sign of Barrett either direction or in the street between the two buildings opposite him. However, the cross street was clogged with people and vehicles, all traffic at a complete standstill. Drivers and passengers were exiting their cars to stare in curiosity and confusion at the blasted building.

Noah approached the nearest bystander and gripped the man's arm. He jumped, startled, and gazed wide-eyed at Noah and his gun. "Sir," Noah said, "the man with the sling - did you see him? Which way did he go?"

The man raised his other arm and pointed down the street behind him. Noah wasted no time, springing into a run, checking every side street and alley he passed. The sound of sirens, honking horns, shouting and screaming people and the frantic radio chatter emitting from Stiles' radio dominated his perception, deafening him to the smaller, more immediate sounds of his own footfalls on the pavement, his labored breathing. And, most importantly, to any sound that might betray Barrett's passage or presence.

He was running blind - both figuratively and half literally, and could feel Barrett slipping through his fingers. He stumbled to a stop and took in his surroundings. There was a promising-looking narrow and shadowy alley across the street to his right. It was littered with overflowing Dumpsters and a haphazard stack of discarded furniture.

He had to concentrate, he told himself as he crossed the street. He paused at the mouth of the alley, gun at the ready. A glance inside it showed no immediate sign of Barrett, so he eased past the worn out loveseat with two broken dining chairs piled on it and entered the alley. He looked at the objects surrounding him, trying to look at each one separately and slowly, the way he had when processing a crime scene. He was having a hard time fighting the feeling that Barrett was behind him, in his blind spot, no matter which way he turned, upsetting his already compromised balance.

He stopped and closed his eyes, taking a deep, cleansing breath and letting it out slowly. He needed to focus on perceiving what seemed beyond his limited senses. Eyes closed, he found a sort of balance he couldn't feel when viewing the world with one eye – while also leaving himself vulnerable and near panic. This is just like the session with Dr. Weymouth...just focus.

He slowed his breathing and his heart rate decreased. He took a few tentative steps further into the alley, noting how his own footsteps sounded to him. He focused hearing past the radio chatter and the street noise, concentrating the way Dr. Weymouth had taught him. He flared his nostrils to take in the scents around him and caught a trace of something sharp and metallic: sweat and blood.

There was a rustle of a plastic bag and a soft metallic click from close by, the sound coming to his right ear at an angle which told him it was from behind and to his left, where the furniture and trash were piled up. It all only took seconds, but left Noah with just a fraction of a second to react. His eyes snapped open as he dropped to the ground. A gunshot rang out above him as he rolled onto his back.

With Stiles' gun gripped in hand, he took aim at the man standing over him and fired.

Tony Barrett crumpled to the dirty pavement, screaming through gritted teeth. His gun lay on the ground, the bloody hand he cradled against his stomach no longer able to wield it. Noah got to his feet and kicked the gun - Bobby Avalon's missing Colt, he'd wager - out of Barrett's reach.

Noah stood looming over Barrett's writhing form, Stiles' gun leveled at the man's head. "Hello, Tony," he said. "That looks like it hurts."

"You can't - you can't be here," he sputtered. "I k-killed you."

"Sorry to disappoint, Tony. By the way, the man you did stab - he didn't die either. Not permanently, anyway."

"Please! You have to understand, I didn't want to kill anyone, but no one was listening... Please, I'm sorry - so sorry." He sucked in a breath and pressed his hand closer to his body. "You have to help me!"

Noah stared at him, this man who had hurt and killed people who dedicated their lives to helping others - who had nearly killed someone Noah loved while intending to kill him instead.

"Okay, Tony," he said. "What would you like me to do?" He pressed the muzzle of the gun against the side of the man's head. "I could end the pain for you now -" Barrett cried out unintelligibly, "-or I could just walk away and let you bleed to death."

He knelt down next to the bloody mess, "Or, I could call in the paramedics and save your worthless life-"

"Yes, please - I need to make you understand!"

"-and let you rot in jail until your hair falls out of your toothless old head or they give you the needle." The two stared at each other a moment. Then Noah stood and brought up Stiles' radio. "Requesting emergency medical services to the alley behind... 1321 Woolworth," he said with a glance at the address stenciled on the Dumpster. "I have the suspect in custody. I repeat: suspect apprehended, 10-52 requested in alley behind 1321 Woolworth. Over."

Stiles appeared at the end of the alley before Noah had ended the transmission. He approached cautiously until he saw Barrett bleeding on the ground. Then he swore under his breath and rushed forward, pulling a handkerchief out of his pocket.

"What the hell, Harkham? Scum's gonna bleed to death before we take him in with you just standing there." He knelt next to Barrett and wrapped the handkerchief around his hand, staunching the blood flow.

Noah didn't answer him. He didn't even look at him. But he lowered the gun and returned it to its non-firing position before dropping it to the ground next to its owner. He walked away, blinking slowly, letting the pent-up adrenaline fade away as he let the radio slip out of his grasp. It landed on a pile of garbage. Stiles called after him, but Noah kept walking.

It was over...

Except it wasn't. He made his way through the dust and debris around the high-rise, searching for Frankie and the others. Cops and rescue personnel blurred past in all directions. Chaos seemed to reign for several moments before he could discern any pattern to their movements.

When he got to Frankie's empty car, he noticed how much he was shaking. He opened the back door and sat on the backseat, facing out, and even here glass and debris crunched under his feet. He ran his hands across his face and hair, trying to occupy them so the trembling ceased.

No sign of his partner anywhere.

Ziehring stood across the street shouting instructions over the radio and to officers as they rushed by. Noah was approaching his former captain before he even realized he had gotten out of the car. "Captain," he said once he reached him, "where are they? Tell me they made it out okay."

Ziehring's face was ashen, his expression a little dazed. "Bastard had a fire bomb," he muttered to himself. "Remote detonated..." He seemed to shake himself mentally and looked at Noah. "Harkham - thank God you got him. Who is this guy?"

"Where's Frankie? Did they get out before it went off?"

"They were in the middle of evacuating. We thought he would just set the place on fire if we caught him - we never expected this. When he wasn't there, I -" he stopped and swallowed, giving his voice a moment to stop quavering, "I sent in CSU."

Noah's gut clenched. "No," he whispered, his breath knocked from him.

"I didn't know... Rescue's looking for their -for them," Ziehring said. "We're still trying to sort this out. Stiles has Barrett with the paramedics now, trying to see if there are any more surprises. Bomb squad's on the way, too, just in case." He paused and shook his head. "I just don't get it. Why this - why any of it? Did he say anything to you?"

Noah thought back. "Yeah. He said he had to do it, but he was sorry. He wanted the chance to make us understand."

"Geez, don't tell me he's going for an insanity plea." Ziehring's radio crackled to life. An urgent voice broke through the static. "-multiple wounded, we need more medics up here -" then the line was consumed by interference.

Noah took a step, but Ziehring put a hand on his chest to stop him from getting any closer to the building. "We'll get them, Harkham," he said, rushing away.

Noah wanted to protest, to demand to be allowed to help, but he now understood he didn't have the right. He didn't have a place in this anymore. So instead, he nodded to himself, watching him go. "You better."

CHAPTER FORTY-THREE

———

WHEN CONRAD CAME TO, his mind felt sluggish and nothing he saw made any sense. He became aware of a steady beeping and the feeling of having lost time. Was he still inside the apartment? There had been fire, an explosion, and choking, dusty smoke, but here he could breathe easily. A glance to his left revealed a thinly shaded window, through which he could see night had fallen. The orange-yellow light from a lamppost picked its way through the seams of the shade, throwing spots of light across the bed he was lying in.

Where am I?

His eyes focused on a shadow at the foot of his bed. It moved and he realized there was someone seated in a chair, watching him. His heart jack-hammered, and he heard the rhythmic beeping increase in correlation. The increased blood flow, in turn, caused a tremendous pounding deep inside his skull. He groaned.

The figure in the chair stirred and stood, and then approached a little unsteadily. "Hey," a familiar voice murmured.

Conrad fought the pain to focus on the shadow. "Neil?" He was surprised at how his voice croaked.

"Yeah, it's me. Do you want me to get a nurse for you?"

He shook his head, which caused stars to burst and fade in the air between them. He held still and closed his eyes a moment. "What happened?"

Neil had moved away from him for a few seconds, but now returned with the chair. He sat as close as he could, and Conrad could see him better now in the dim light. "You got a pretty nasty whack to the head. Your skull fractured and they had to remove a small sliver from your brain."

"What?" The beeping increased a little again.

"You're going to be fine. There was some swelling, so they had to keep you asleep until it went down." He paused a moment. "It's been three days."

"Three days?"

"You've been in and out some today, but this is the first time you've been fully lucid." Neil's brow scrunched in a frown. "You had us worried."

"Now you know how it feels," he replied with a small chuckle. He put a hand to his aching head and suppressed another groan. "Tell me they found Barrett."

Neil smirked. "He's in jail. We got him. Well, actually, Noah did."

"Good. There was an explosion...a fire," he said, almost more a question than a statement.

"Yeah. Barrett had a remote detonated fire bomb. They think Sammy the Stitch may have helped him put it together, but he's not talking."

"The others?"

"Cox broke a couple ribs. Adelmo broke his wrist. They both got a few minor burns, too. Branson was lucky. He was halfway back down the fire escape when it went off. He took a tumble and got pretty banged up, but it could have been a lot worse. Frankie -" his voice faltered a little but he forged ahead. "They say he's going to be fine, but he got some pretty bad burns. He was trapped under a section of the ceiling that collapsed from the fire. Second degree on his arms and chest. He's in the burn unit now."

"Dear God..." He was almost afraid to ask his next question, but he did anyway. "And Parker?"

"Parker is, uh - he's not so good, Con."

He swallowed past the constriction in his throat. "Tell me."

"I'm not sure what it was, but something struck him in the back. And the blast wave, uh, tore up one of his legs. They took him in for surgery, but..." he paused and looked down. When he looked back up at Conrad, there were tears in his eyes and one fell down his face. "There was too much damage to his spine."

Conrad's blood went cold. "What are you telling me?"

"They say he's never going to walk again."

CHAPTER FORTY-FOUR

———

"I DON'T UNDERSTAND why you aren't getting this," Barrett made an impatient gesture at Ziehring and the crumpled, bloodstained paper that lay on the Interview Room table between them. "It's all right there."

"Forgive me if I'm having a hard time understanding why you think this," Ziehring tapped a finger on the evidence bag containing the paper, "gives you the right to attack and kill innocent people."

Barrett shook his head. "No, I never wanted to kill anyone. I never intended to hurt anyone, but no one would listen to what I was telling you. None of you wanted to see what happened - how you failed."

Ziehring took a breath before replying, trying to quell the frustration bubbling inside. "How we failed. How did we fail, Tony?"

"All those people - the kids! I tried to stop it; I tried to get someone to come, to keep it from happening." He leaned across the table, tapping his chest with a finger of his bandaged hand while the cast on his other arm knocked against the table's edge. "I even tried to get him the money, to make him change his mind. He said it wasn't enough and he couldn't wait. I told him I wouldn't do it. So he did it himself." He squeezed his eyes shut and wiped his bandaged hand across his mouth, stifling a sob.

He was jittery, nervous; he kept jouncing his legs and fidgeting with his bandage and cast. When he opened his red-rimmed eyes, he stared vacantly at his shaking hands. He seemed more alert today, stronger after a blood-transfusion and short hospital stay, but his state of mind was still a little questionable.

"All I could do was watch it go up," he said, his voice flat and dull as lead. "I made the call, but no one came, so I left. I couldn't stand to watch anymore. It was so... ugly. Inelegant." He glanced at Ziehring, almost apologetically.

"What do you mean, you tried to tell us? How? Why didn't anyone come?"

Barrett scoffed. "I did what I thought was right - I called 911. I told you it was going to happen, but not one of you came to stop it." He gave Ziehring a look of pure wrath. "No one came until it was too late. You all let them die. It's on you, all of it." He flung a hand in a wide gesture. "So I had to make you see, had to make it right. Someone had to avenge them." He banged his gunshot hand on the table and Ziehring involuntarily flinched. Barrett seemed not to notice the pain.

"All you did was kill and injure innocent people," Ziehring replied, gritting his teeth. "You are a murderer, a maimer, just like Simon Turner."

"Don't you dare compare me to him," Barrett warned in a terribly quiet voice. The image of a caged lion sprang into Ziehring's mind at the sound of it.

He decided to change tack. "You are aware we have Simon Turner in custody for the Brookview fire, aren't you, Mr. Barrett?"

He snorted derisively. "Like he's ever going to be indicted. That case is tainted."

Ziehring felt a shock bolt through him. "What are you talking about? We've got him cold."

Barrett gave him a look. "Cold," he scoffed. "Maybe you would if the evidence were admissible. Maybe you would if he would confess. But while he's got one of your own in his pocket and a lock on his tongue, he'll be back in his penthouse in no time. Or, at least," he added, "once the contractors get the place put back together."

Ziehring decided to let the flippant comment slide and focus on the real problem. "Mr. Turner is a very powerful man, but I sincerely doubt any of our officers would help him get away with arson and murder."

He shrugged. "You paint a picture green enough, you can cover up any amount of red."

"That's very poetic, Tony, but where's the proof? Tangible evidence. Do you have any?"

"What happened after I called 911? I'd say, start there. When you figure that out, and when you get it in writing that I can take the stand and tell the whole story, without interruption, before the jury and the press, I'll give you all the proof you need."

Ziehring eyed him a moment. "That's up to the DA," he said, "but I'll see if I can make it happen. Sit tight." He got up from the table and left the interrogation room to join Gerald Warner in the adjoining observation room. He stood frowning at the glass, his arms crossed.

"First thing I recommend is a psychiatric evaluation," Warner said.

"He seems sane enough to me," Ziehring said, watching Barrett through the glass. "Agitated, angry and driven by guilt and grief, yes, but it sounds like he knows exactly what he did and what's going on."

"Perhaps, but I want the evaluation done anyway. If he passes, there is no possibility the defense can try for an insanity or diminished capacity plea."

"All right," he sighed. "I'll call in the psychologist. But what about the rest of it? Should we be willing to deal?"

"Well," Warner mused, his eyebrows drawn together over his pale brown eyes, "that depends."

"On what?"

"On whether or not he's right about Turner's case. The motion to suppress the arson kit collected by CSU from Turner Heights has been submitted, but the judge is waiting on the outcome of the Internal Affairs investigation to decide whether to grant it or not. But seeing as the subject of the investigation -"

"Neil Coates," Ziehring supplied.

"Yes. Since Mr. Coates is still hospitalized, the hearing is postponed until his release."

"I'm sure Neil is so sorry for the inconvenience, Counselor," Ziehring retorted.

Warner lifted a hand. "You know that's not what I meant. I simply mean that until we know the outcome, we shouldn't be in any rush to negotiate. We have to ask ourselves what his game is."

"What could it hurt?" Ziehring posed. "All he wants is to exercise his right to address the court in his own defense."

"What he wants is a soapbox," Warner countered. "He could bring a whole lot of fire down on this precinct, not to mention the fire department and hospital system. You heard him, he wants to lay all of this at your feet."

"Let him try. The jury should be intelligent enough to see reality. And the reality is this man murdered a nurse and attempted to murder a firefighter, a criminalist and several law enforcement personnel. He's wreaked a lot of havoc."

"Yes, he has. Which is why he's not my first choice for a star witness against Turner," Warner wearily rubbed his forehead. "We have a case against Turner. Even if it's shaky, I can sell it. Even without the arson kit evidence. And, now that we have Barrett's statement, you may be able to get a confession out of Turner."

Ziehring frowned. "That would be a long shot, Gerald."

"It's worth a try," he shrugged.

Ziehring sighed. This whole thing was getting too complicated for his liking. He opened the door and told the officer guarding the interview room door to take Barrett back to lockup. As the officer escorted him out of the room, Barrett saw Warner leaving.

"Wait, please, I need to speak to the Captain," Barrett asked the officer. "Captain?"

"What do you want, Barrett?"

"Did you get it? Will I be allowed to address the court?"

"I don't have an answer for you yet." He started to walk away.

"Wait!" Barrett commanded. "I have the right to tell the story. If you won't let me do it in a court of law, I'll do it in the court of public opinion. The press will love to know I'm being denied my Constitutional right to speak on my own behalf at trial and defend myself."

Ziehring turned back and charged toward Barrett. "Listen to me, you son of a bitch," he said, all but snarling with anger, "don't you talk to me about what you deserve. My men almost died because of you. You hurt a lot of innocent people, killed an innocent woman, because you think we are responsible for the people Turner killed? What makes you think you deserve anything other than the needle? You should be thanking whatever god scum like you pray to that you even have the privilege of a fair trial, because real justice would have been for you to die in that alley in a pool of what little blood you had left in you." He stopped before he lost further control. "Get him out of here," he ordered the officer.

"You can't let Turner get away with this," Barrett yelled as he was practically dragged down the hallway. "You need me, Ziehring!"

CHAPTER FORTY-FIVE

———

TWO DAYS LATER, NEIL sat in an uncomfortable wooden chair at a table in a small room that would make a prison cell seem light and cheery. The light was dim and the air too close, making it feel even smaller. Across the room, at a larger table, three grim-looking men sat facing him.

Thomas Ashton, Neil's boss, sat furthest right. His thinning hair was neatly cropped, his long face somber - as was his suit. He looked like he was attending a funeral. That didn't bode well.

To the left was the investigator from Special Services-Internal Affairs, Inspector Jordan Ellis. He was about as conservative and nondescript as a person could be, which was probably deliberate. As if humanity and personality would get in the way of his job. He occupied the second to last seat; the furthest one left was where Cal Parker would have sat if they had delayed the hearing until he was out of the hospital.

Directly in front of Neil, between the two other men, sat a man he'd never met before. He'd been introduced as Judge Richard Andersen, and he would act as arbiter to the proceedings. With no direct tie to either the lab or to Internal Affairs, it could only be presumed he was to be an impartial party to this farce. Whether or not this was true remained to be seen.

Jordan Ellis cleared his throat, then coolly eyed Neil. "Mr. Coates, we have before us here a very... sticky situation. Serious allegations have been leveled at you; and, even though the source of those allegations is himself facing serious charges, that does not diminish the enormity of the situation." He paused a moment, then, with an officious air, announced, "You have been accused of planting evidence, entrapment and assault."

He shuffled some papers lying before him. "We have the results of your polygraph examination," he said, his eyes flicking to Ashton, who was wearing the slightest of frowns. "We have also interviewed various members of the team involved in the Turner/Brookview arson investigation, as well as a select few of your other colleagues. It might please you to know you are highly regarded in both the crime lab and the Fifth Precinct." He gave Neil a patronizing smile. "However, high regard has no bearing on guilt or innocence, does it?"

Neil's eyes narrowed fractionally. "All due respect, sir," he said, "what exactly is it you need from me if you already have statements and the polygraph results?"

"We just need to hear the whole story, start to finish," Ashton answered for him. "In your own words. There are a few minor points left to be cleared up."

"Where would you like me to start, sir?"

"Let's go back to the first day of the investigation," Ellis said. "The Fire Chief called in the arson, Detectives Harkham and Franks were dispatched to the scene. How is it you, too, came to be on scene that day?"

Neil took a breath before answering. "Detective Sergeant Harkham and Detective Franks called the lab and spoke with Cal Parker," he couldn't help glancing at the empty chair. "They requested someone from the lab to help with processing the evidence and to search for clues as to the subject's movements after committing the crime. I was sent. A few uniform officers were also called in to help with this and canvassing the area for witnesses or anyone who might be able to provide more information."

"Did Parker specifically ask you to be the one who went?" Ashton asked.

Neil nodded. "He did. I've worked a few arson cases in my career and was familiar with the procedures."

Ellis flipped through the papers. "You worked the Woodbridge fire a few years ago, is that correct?"

He considered the question a moment before answering. "I did. Among many others."

"And the outcome of that investigation was...what?"

"Unsolved."

"Unsolved," Ellis mused. "And the reason for that was?"

"Insufficient evidence." Neil had no choice but to answer, but he was only going to answer what was asked, offering no more than necessary.

"All right," Ellis said, "so you were selected for this assignment. Did you often work cases alongside your cousin, Detective Harkham?"

"Occasionally." Neil glanced at the judge, Andersen, and noticed he had a small smile on his lips as he gave Neil an almost imperceptible nod.

"The lab is a bit short-staffed, Inspector, as is the police department," Ashton supplied. "On the rare occasion, Mr. Coates and Detective Sergeant Harkham would wind up working the same case. But you are no doubt aware of Harkham's unique arrangement with the CSU."

"Yes." Ellis almost sneered the word. "It is a rather unique position, as you say. Not often does a detective have license to act outside his purview."

"Mister Harkham holds a degree in Forensic Science," Ashton said. "He was granted license, as you say, to put his skills and knowledge to a practical use. Protocols and chain of custody were always adhered to with extreme strictness, as assured by myself and Captain Ziehring." He made a curt gesture. "Harkham's career is not in question here."

"No, just his cousin's," Ellis replied. "I suggest we continue with the hearing, then. Mr. Coates, tell us what happened once you arrived on the scene."

"I got to the Brookview building and was briefed on the situation by both the Fire Chief and Detective Franks. They requested my help sorting through the debris to locate any and all items that could contain traces of the accelerant the Chief had found at the point of origin or any other evidence of arson. If it turned out what is termed the 'arson kit' was not on the premises, I was to help in the search for it in the surrounding areas."

He cleared his throat. "Usually, an arson kit consists of the container used to transport and deliver the accelerant to the scene, as well as the vehicle by which the fire was started, such as a lighter, book of matches, that sort of thing."

"And was this arson kit found at the scene?"

He cleared his throat again. It was still a little uncomfortable to speak, but the wound to his throat was healing rather well. "No, it was not. Approximately half an hour after I finished processing the crime scene, and it was determined the kit was not on scene, I - along with Officers

Daniel Branson and Kenneth Stiles - started searching the Dumpsters, alleys and sewer grates in the surrounding areas. It was believed the arsonist took it with him to dispose of elsewhere, and may have dumped it as he fled."

Ellis made some notes on the papers in front of him. "But the kit was not recovered from any of these places that were searched."

"No, sir, it was not."

He kept writing, but made a gesture with the pen at one point. "Go on."

"Not long after we started the search, I noticed there was a man watching us from up the block. He was dressed in a long overcoat, like a trench coat, even though it was too warm for it that day, and he was wearing sunglasses. After several seconds, he went to a pay phone and made a call, watching us the whole time. At first, I thought he was probably a reporter or something."

"What did you do at this point?"

"I pointed him out to Officer Stiles, but he didn't think anything of it, except he was probably a reporter, like I said. We continued to search the area - I was searching the sewer grates, he was checking the Dumpsters. I kept noticing the guy in the phone booth, though. The way he kept watching us was becoming more suspicious. So I radioed Detective Franks, told him about the man in the phone booth and said I felt I should check him out. Detective Franks agreed and said he was on his way and wanted to speak to the man as well."

His voice was getting raspy. He was never particularly verbose, and after the attack, he had been instructed to rest his voice more than usual. It was getting a strenuous workout today. He took a sip of water from the glass on his table and rested just a moment before continuing.

"Apparently, the man could guess what we were planning, because as soon as I put my radio back on my belt, he hung up the phone and exited the phone booth. I called out to him, identified myself as being from the crime lab and asked him to stop, but he ignored me and nearly ran up the block away from me. I started to pursue him, but since he already had such a lead on me, I decided to find out who he had been talking to."

"You contacted the operator and got the number dialed from the phone, is that correct?"

"I did. I identified myself and requested the number last dialed from the payphone and the name of the person it was registered to."

"But you did not have a warrant."

Neil suppressed his frustration. "I felt it was highly likely the man had been in contact with the arsonist and that evidence may be destroyed as a result. I felt this was a case of exigent circumstances, which negated the need for a warrant. I reported what I saw and what I did to Detective Franks. He supported my decision."

Ellis looked like he was making a mental note of that, but did not write anything down. "And Detective Harkham and Officers Branson and Stiles? Did they agree?"

"Detective Sergeant Harkham was canvassing for witnesses. Officer Stiles was searching Dumpsters a few streets over by then. I was told Officer Branson had received a phone call and had gone to the squad car to take it privately."

"I see," Ellis said. "Who did the man call? To whom did the phone number belong?"

"Simon Turner," Neil answered. "Turner was already at the top of our list of suspects, as the owner of the property and holder of the insurance policy, so it wasn't really a surprise someone would be keeping tabs on the investigation for him. Detective Franks decided to pick Mister Turner up for questioning, and he asked me and Officer Branson to accompany him in order to search the area around his building for the arson kit. Detective Sergeant Harkham and Officer Stiles would stay behind and continue the search in the areas surrounding the crime scene."

"Just to be clear: you were only going to search the public areas around the building, correct?"

"Correct."

"Because you did not have a search warrant for Mr. Turner's home or anywhere inside the Turner Heights building."

"That's right."

Ellis made another note. "What happened when you arrived at the Turner Heights building?"

"Detective Franks proceeded to Mr. Turner's residence to take him into custody. Officer Branson and I had split up to search different areas outside the building. I was finished searching one side of the building and came around to the back alley. I didn't realize it, but Officer Branson was already searching this area..." Neil paused as something about the memory nagged at him. "Branson was near the Dumpster by the back door," he continued slowly. "His back was to the door. Mr. Turner was standing in the alley behind him."

He paused again, frowning. "Turner was holding a canvas bag, which appeared to be smudged with soot -"

"I'm sorry," Ellis interrupted, "but how far away from Mr. Turner and Officer Branson were you at this point?"

"I was about halfway down the alley, approximately a couple dozen yards," Neil replied.

"And you were able to tell the bag was smudged with soot, specifically?" He raised an eyebrow. "Impressive."

Neil took and released a couple breaths before answering to give himself a moment to master his irritation. "It was a light colored canvas bag and there were large, irregular patches of a dark grey substance that were clearly visible. They were the same color as the soot smudges on my Tyvek jumpsuit and gloves. So, the smudges were consistent with soot, but, no, I could not tell definitively they were, in fact, soot. Which is why I said it *appeared* to be smudged with soot."

"Proceed, Mr. Coates," Ashton said with a sharp look at Ellis. Judge Andersen looked away, a grin on his face that he tried to hide.

"As I was saying, Turner was standing behind Branson. He was about ten feet away, with the canvas bag in hand. I called out a warning to Branson, and, when he turned around, Turner hit him in the face with the bag. Branson went down and the bag fell out of Turner's hands, and he turned and ran. I was already in pursuit and caught up to Turner just after he exited the alley and started up the sidewalk of the intersecting street. I made a grab for him and we struggled, wherein he tried to hit me in the face as well. I restrained him, advising him Branson was going to bring him in for questioning. I asked him to cooperate with us to make it better for himself."

He took another sip of water before continuing. "He tried to run, so I grabbed for him again. He overbalanced and fell, striking the corner of the mailbox with the side of his face. I helped him to his feet and tried to assess the cut, but he started yelling that I had planted the arson kit in his building, then called him saying we were on the way to pick him and the evidence up. He said I tricked him into getting caught with the evidence. And he said I had deliberately pushed him into the mailbox, that I was trying to kill him. He started throwing out words like entrapment, assault, illegal search and seizure, that sort of thing."

"Well, at least we can dismiss the part about Neil making the call because Officer Stiles confirmed seeing the man in the phone booth as well," Ashton said.

"Yes," Ellis agreed. "Although there was no one around between the time you say the man fled the area and when you called the operator."

Neil made a slow blink. "You think I really did make the call."

"I don't think one way or another on the matter, Mr. Coates," Ellis said, though the slight smirk on his bland lips seemed to indicate otherwise. "I am merely stating the fact that you have no witnesses or other means to prove your version of events as told here today."

"My version -?" He stopped himself from saying anything heated. Instead, he paused for just a moment, then said in as calm a voice as possible, "I would have thought the sworn statement of an officer of the law and a clear polygraph would be sufficient to counter the accusations of a man who had burned down a building while its inhabitants slept."

He was trying to maintain a cool demeanor, but his emotions were flaring. The increase in his heart rate was making the blood pound in his temples. His head was starting to swim and a bad headache was creeping through his skull. It was long past time he was back home, resting.

"Moving on," Ellis said. "Where was Officer Branson when Mr. Turner had this accident with the mailbox?"

Neil could actually hear quotation marks around the word accident. Didn't think one way or another on the matter, yeah, right. "He had just caught up with us after radioing Detective Franks to bring his car around to pick Turner up."

"But he did not see Mr. Turner trip and hit the mailbox?"

Neil suppressed a frustrated sigh. "He did not, as you know. He came around the corner as I was helping Turner to his feet. Just as Turner started making his accusations."

"So, once again, you unfortunately have no one to back up your story."

Neil gripped the arms of his chair and bit back a sharp retort. He forced himself to take another drink of water, then glared at the Ellis' bland, automaton face. "Neither does Simon Turner. Did you even bother to polygraph him? Or am I the only one being treated like a criminal here?"

"Neil," Ashton warned.

"No, sir - I have had enough of this." His eyes felt like they were on fire and he was nearly trembling with the effort of not shouting. "I did nothing wrong, and certainly nothing illegal. I cannot believe this whole thing has gone this far. Why is it so easy for everyone to question my word - the word of someone who has dedicated an entire career to the truth? Why is it Turner's accusations were responded to by launching a thorough investigation into my career and my actions instead of with disbelief and dismissal?"

There was an unexpected knock on the door to the little room, making everyone jump a little and somewhat dispelling the tension. Ashton rose and went to open the door, where he spoke in hushed tones with the unseen person on the other side. A moment later, he closed the door and returned to the table, a file folder in hand.

"Pardon the interruption, Judge Andersen, Inspector Ellis," Ashton said as he sat down. "I have something here that should be of interest to everyone." He raised his gaze to Neil briefly, but in that short moment, Neil saw a glint of excitement in his boss' eyes.

"What is it, Ashton?" Ellis demanded.

"I have the transcript of the recorded conversation between Mr. Turner and Mr. Barrett just minutes before Mr. Turner was apprehended by Mr. Coates and Officer Branson."

"Excuse me?" Ellis sounded incredulous, which was almost exactly how Neil was feeling, though, he figured, for different reasons.

"You were told yesterday Tony Barrett had confessed to calling Simon Turner and telling him the cops were onto him. That he had told Turner he knew where the evidence was and would take the cops to it if Turner didn't turn himself in."

"Wait, what?" Neil asked. If Ellis knew this, why were they even here going through the motions?

Ashton glanced at Neil, then turned back to Ellis. "You said you needed proof in order to clear Neil in this matter. I have it right here." He held up the folder.

"May I see that, Mr. Ashton?" Judge Andersen held a hand toward Ashton, who gave him the folder with a nod. Andersen skimmed the enclosed transcript. "Barrett: They know it was you. And I know where you stashed the evidence. Turner: Who is this? Barrett: Tell them what you've done. I'm going to take them to the proof if you don't turn yourself in, confess to murdering all those people. Turner: I don't know what you're talking about, pal, but I suggest you mind your own business. Barrett: This is my business. Or have you forgotten so quickly? Have you forgotten how you asked me to get you out of your mess, how you wouldn't let me do it the right way, the safe way and did it yourself? Turner is silent for several seconds, then says: Tony?"

Andersen laid the transcript aside and turned to Inspector Ellis. "Is that sufficient, Inspector? There is more I could read if not."

Ellis cleared his throat, looking uncomfortable. "No, Your Honor, that will suffice - if it satisfies you, sir."

"Indeed it does. All right, Mr. Coates," Andersen said, "if you wouldn't mind waiting outside a moment."

"Your Honor," Ellis argued, "we'll need more than a moment to render a verdict on this."

"We'll send for you when we've come to an agreement," Andersen told Neil, ignoring Ellis.

Neil stood and swayed with fatigue. He steadied himself with a hand on the back of the chair. He hadn't regained all of his strength yet and still tired quickly, something he had been able to disguise until now. A couple of steadying breaths and he could open his eyes without the room tilting.

"Are you all right?" Ashton asked.

"Fine. I just..." Something about the image he had replayed in his mind earlier now clicked. "Oh, no..." He reran the scenario, just to be sure. There it was: the slight turn of the head, the incriminating body language that told the story he hadn't picked up on before.

"Neil?" Ashton half rose from his chair.

He looked up. "I have one last question: why is it Simon Turner didn't run when he first saw Officer Branson? Why was he *with* him in the alley?"

Ellis scrunched his features in puzzlement. "Excuse me?"

"When I first walked into the alley, why was Simon Turner just standing there, near a police officer with incriminating evidence in his hands? Why would he think he had no reason to run - until he saw me?"

Andersen smiled. "Thank you, Mr. Coates. We will certainly pursue this line of inquiry. I believe Mr. Warner is in the hall. Would you be so kind as to send him in on your way out?"

Neil nodded and caught Ashton's eye as he turned to leave. It almost looked like his boss was feeling a bit vindicated. If that were the case, if he had been in Neil's corner this whole time, Neil felt a slight temperature change toward the man.

Out in the hall, he saw Gerald Warner pacing with nervous energy. When he saw Neil exit the room, he came up to him without delay. "They wouldn't let me in while you were in there. What happened? What did they say?"

"They are deliberating. But I think they may have set their sights on other prey."

Warner looked shocked. "What? Did someone already tell them what Barrett said?"

Neil slightly furrowed his brow. "What?

"Never mind. I'll fill you in later, if it turns out to be true." He glanced past Neil to the door. "I better get in there before they get any further." With that, he rushed past him and entered the room, leaving Neil to try to figure out what had just happened.

CHAPTER FORTY-SIX

———

"YOU WANTED TO SEE ME, Captain?" Noah asked as he rapped his knuckles on the door to Ziehring's office.

The Captain looked up from his paperwork. "Yes. Come in and close the door."

Harkham closed the door behind him and settled into the chair opposite his former boss. Ziehring continued to fill out the forms for a few moments while Noah waited in silence. At length, he set aside the papers and looked at Noah with an odd expression. "How well do you know Daniel Branson?"

Whatever he might have been expecting, this was not it. "He's worked support on a lot of cases I've handled. He always seemed pretty competent and professional, you know, intelligent, thorough..." His voice trailed off. "What exactly is this about, if I may ask, sir?"

"During the investigation of the Brookview fire, did he say or do anything that seemed," he rolled his palm upward, "odd or unusual at all?"

"Sir? I'm not sure what you're asking me here."

"Please, Noah, just - did you notice anything strange?"

He thought back. "Not really," he said with a shrug. "I mean, after the initial response to the scene, most of the officers went back to other duties, but Branson volunteered to stay on and help. I was processing the scene most of the time, and then Branson went with Neil and Frankie to Turner Heights to pick up Simon Turner, so I didn't spend much time with him that day."

But then he remembered, "At one point he got a phone call and left the scene to take it. That's why Neil called Stiles over to check out the guy in the phone booth instead of Branson. He was only gone for a few minutes, though. He was back in time for Frankie to take him to the Heights."

Ziehring frowned. "So he left the scene in the middle of the investigation."

"I wouldn't say he left, sir. Neil said he just walked up the block to the squad car." Noah narrowed his eyes. "Sir, what is all this? What's going on?"

Ziehring sighed. "Barrett claimed Turner has had a cop in his pocket for a long time. He says that's why the case would never be prosecuted and why he felt the need to take it upon himself to 'seek justice.'"

Noah's eyebrows shot upwards. "And you think it's Branson?"

"We know it was," Ziehring nodded. "Internal Affairs has stepped in. Neil actually put it together for them before they even heard Barrett's accusation. They pulled his financial records and there was some... suspicious activity. It didn't take long for Branson to admit it when we confronted him." He sighed.

"His wife has been battling some serious illness for several years," Ziehring continued, "and the medical bills were getting too much for them, so he took out a 'loan' from Turner. The poor fool thought being a cop would mean he could keep Turner in check, but all it did was put him under Turner's thumb instead. He's been in a jam for a couple years, couldn't see a way out." He frowned. "I think he was relieved it's over."

Noah let out a slow breath as he thought this over. "I never would have thought he would be dirty. Especially not enough to help someone cover up murder." He ran a hand across his mouth, then turned his palm up in a shrug-like gesture. "Guess that shows how little people can know each other... Does this mean anything for Neil? Does it help?"

"Ellis has yet to announce the official verdict, but he will be cleared. Turner recanted the allegations once he found out Branson rolled on him and Barrett had recorded their conversation."

"Excellent. Does this mean the arson kit will be admissible?"

Ziehring shook his head, his expression one of frustration. "I don't know yet."

"Well, maybe you don't even need it. With Branson talking - and Barrett - maybe Turner will just roll over and plead guilty. Make it easy on everyone." He was still finding this hard to believe. Daniel Branson... "Sir, Branson may have disgraced the uniform, but he's trying to make it right now. What's going to happen to him?"

"He's lost his job, of course, but it still remains to be seen exactly how many laws he broke helping Turner. All I know of right now is he filed a false report after responding to Barrett's 911 call - and he somehow managed to make the recording of the call disappear. He claims he didn't know the building was occupied and thought he was just facilitating insurance fraud, not murder. It's going to be quite the mess for Gerald and the IA boys to untangle."

They fell silent a moment. Then Noah asked, "Have you heard any updates on everyone yet?"

"Uhh, Cox and Adelmo will be on desk duty until they heal up some more, but they'll be back tomorrow. Franks is due back in a couple of weeks. He declined to take his full leave."

Noah smiled. "Of course."

"I spoke to Neil earlier. He's been released and is due back to work Monday, as you probably already know."

"Yeah."

"Conrad is supposed to be back to work Monday, once all the neurological testing is done. Ashton says they think everything will be fine, though." He paused a moment. "Nobody has heard anything about Parker. Word is he's refusing to see anyone."

"I can understand that," Noah said in a subdued voice. He could somewhat imagine what the man must be going through.

Ziehring was searching Noah's face, as if trying to decide whether or not to say what he was thinking. After a moment, however, the decision seemed to have been made. "I asked you here for another reason, too, Noah. I... I wanted to apologize."

Noah furrowed his brow. "For what?"

"I underestimated you. I've known you for over twelve years, even before you made Detective Squad, and I still listened to doctors and the higher ups instead of trusting what I knew to be true about you. You handled yourself remarkably well out there today, just like you always had done... before. So, I'm sorry."

Noah swallowed. "Thank you, sir," he said in a small voice.

"I wish to God I could give you your shield back and send you back out there. I can't," he said with genuine sounding regret. "But what I can do is offer you a job. A different one."

"Sir?"

"The Powers That Be have implemented a broader selection of continuing education programs for law enforcement officials. Basically, there are new mandatory and elective courses available several times a year for the uniformed and detective ranks. Most are offered at the campus or online, but some have instructors who will visit the precincts. I was... hoping you would accept an in-house instructor's position."

"I - I don't know what to say," he said. Nothing about this visit had been predictable.

"You would be able to design the curriculum, tailor the course to your own specifications. The salary would be a little less, I'm afraid, but you'd have benefits and you've got your pension, too, of course. And anything you need, I'll make sure you get." He paused, assessing him. "What do you say, Harkham?"

"Captain, before I say anything, tell me something - straight, no B.S."

"Okay."

"Do you feel sorry for me?"

Ziehring opened his mouth, then shut it with a slight frown. After a moment, he said, "I did. At first. But now?" He shook his head. "Not at all. The...incident changed you, Noah. It almost broke you, I know, but somehow, you've got your fight back. The same drive I saw in you every day on the job. Maybe even more than before." He smiled. "So, no, I don't feel sorry for you. I do feel a little bit sorry for the crooks your students will collar, but what can I say?" he added with a little laugh.

Noah smiled. "Would I have my own office?"

"If that's what you want."

"Would I be able to make anyone not up to par stand in front of the class wearing a straw hat and sing, 'If I only had a brain'?"

"We may have to discuss that one," Ziehring said, chuckling. "Does this mean you're in?"

Noah thought it over. "Yes, sir," he said, smiling. "I'm in."

CHAPTER FORTY-SEVEN

———

NEIL WALKED INTO THE ballistics lab the following Monday afternoon as Robin's text requested, but no one was in sight. He frowned. "Robin?"

"Yeah, I'll be right there." Her voice came from the Exemplar Room in the back, where she kept all the sample weapons and ammunition. A moment later she stepped out, a big smile lighting up her face when she saw him. "Neil, you came," she said, and before he knew it, she had crossed the room and caught him up in a fierce hug. "It is so good to see you back."

"Thanks," he managed to say.

She let go suddenly and stepped back. "Sorry! I didn't mean to crush you. I get a little too 'happy dog' sometimes." She blushed, then fixed him with a look, an excited gleam in her eyes. "Are you ready?"

"For...what? Your text was pretty vague."

She grabbed his right hand and placed it to cover his eyes. "Keep that there," she instructed, taking his left hand in both of hers and leading him toward the door, "and follow me."

He stumbled along with her out of the ballistics lab. "And we're doing what, exactly?"

"There's something I want you to see," she said, turning him in the hall and walking him toward the direction of the Layout Rooms and the break room beyond. A few moments later, she slowed and then stopped.

"Okay, wait here. No peeking." He heard a door open in front of him and she let go of his arm. "Now you can look."

He opened his eyes to see the break room had been decorated with streamers. He entered the room further and saw a large cake sitting on the table in the middle of the room. The message scrawled in gel icing read: "Welcome back" on one line and "Congratulations" on the second. Robin stood next to him with an expectant smile and holding a pair of plastic cups.

"What's all this?" He asked, deeply touched and stunned.

"Surprise," she said, offering him one of the cups. He took it and discovered it was filled with some sort of punch, which he guessed was from the large glass bowl a little further down from the cake.

"Thanks."

"This is for you, too," she said, and picked up a large gift box from a chair next to the table. "Oh, right," she said with a sheepish grin and took the cup back for a moment to free his hands.

He took the box, and inside found a set of newspaper clippings, mounted and matted in a sleek black frame. The first article bore the headline "County Crime Lab Investigator Cleared of All Charges." The second was from today's paper and the headline read "Suspect Charged in Recent Attacks, Cold Case Arson and More." Neil was particularly pleased with that one, as it marked the end of his hunt for the Woodbridge Center arsonist.

Neil smiled at her. "Thank you. This is... beyond great." He gave her a hug. "All of this, the cake..."

"Would be even better if we actually ate it instead of just staring at it," came a voice from the doorway behind them. They turned to see Conrad Ward grinning at them.

"What are you doing here?" Neil asked, surprised and glad to see him.

Ward clapped him on the shoulder. "Nice to see you, too, man." He turned to Robin. "Shots," he said, holding out his arms for a hug. She smiled and embraced him. He said something to her that Neil couldn't quite hear, but sounded something like, 'he feels the same.'

Neil frowned. What did that mean? Did Conrad figure out - no, no one knew how he felt about Robin, right? Not even he himself, really. Except to say she was the one thing he kept thinking about after he got stabbed, and when he woke up from surgery...

Conrad released Robin and turned to the table. "Screw everybody else, let's carve this beast up!"

He cut the cake into large pieces and passed one to each of them. Robin set hers aside for a moment to present Conrad with his owned framed article. This one was about the aftermath of the explosion and featured a few quotes from Conrad himself. He seemed surprised and touched by the gesture, just like Neil had been. Robin had a way of making people feel cared about, no doubt.

Soon enough, their other colleagues began to drift in to join them, including Tyler Hendricks, Simon Lewis and Jake Saddler. Everyone was talking and laughing before long. Even the usually gruff and grumpy Lewis seemed to be enjoying himself.

Then the door opened again and a wave of silence flowed over the group.

Cal Parker sat in a wheelchair in the doorway. He seemed to have aged ten years in the last few days. His genial face was now haggard and there were dark hollows under his eyes. He regarded them all with an almost cadaverous look. "Doesn't anyone work in this place?"

Some smiled a bit nervously, others muttered things like welcome back and good to see you, and although he seemed aware of them all, his gaze was locked on Conrad. Something almost tangible passed between them, a wave of unspoken disagreement and challenge. It wasn't exactly hostile, just tense.

"Hey, Bossa Nova," Robin said. "You didn't tell us you were coming back today. Cake?"

Parker flicked his gaze to her and his expression softened a little. "No, thank you, Robin. I won't be staying. I just came by to pick up a few things."

"They said you had at least another week in the hospital," Conrad said to him.

"Yes, well, I think I know what's going to be better for me than anyone else does." His eyes hardened again as he looked back at Conrad.

Conrad rolled his eyes and scoffed. "This again."

"Yes, Con. This again. Just let it go."

"Don't do this, Parker," he said, almost pleading.

"Stop acting like a petulant child," Parker snapped.

Nobody moved or spoke. Neil watched the exchange with bated breath. What was going on here?

"Stop being an ass," Conrad countered.

Neil laid a hand on his arm. "You trying to lose your job?" he cautioned.

"Oh, no, he can't fire me," Conrad said, shrugging Neil's hand off. He raised his voice so the whole room could hear. "Didn't you know? He's given up. He quit."

"Quit? I don't understand," Neil said in disbelief.

"You can't be serious," Robin said. She turned to Parker. "Boss?"

"I've made my decision," Parker said to Conrad, ignoring everyone else. "You don't have to agree with it or like it or even understand it. I'm sorry you don't, but that doesn't change anything. I wanted to come here and take my leave of each of you quietly, to end my career on a dignified note."

He tore his glare from Conrad and looked around at those gathered there. "That didn't play out the way I had hoped. So, all I can do now is tell you all how much I have loved my job and all of my employees and that I will-" his voice broke and he stopped a moment.

He took a breath, and when he continued, his voice still trembled. "I will miss each and every one of you. Truly."

He took a moment to look each of them in the eye. Jake Saddler unabashedly shed a tear and Simon Lewis looked like he'd been punched in the gut. Conrad looked... crushed. When it was his turn, Neil felt like Parker's gaze was piercing his heart and it was all he could do not to look away. Parker favored Robin with a sad smile and said, "Good bye."

Then he turned his wheelchair around and left the room. Everyone was still in too much shock to move - until Conrad slammed his plastic cup down on the table, sloshing punch all over himself, and cursed under his breath. He stormed out of the break room, through the door in the back wall. Everyone else milled around a few moments, then started leaving the room with muttered excuses.

"I guess that officially puts an end to the party," Neil said, his voice shaking a bit. It was just he and Robin left now, and she turned wide, glistening eyes to him. He gave her a consoling smile and put his arm around her, pulling her into a hug.

"I'm sorry about your party," she said.

"Don't worry about that," he murmured. "I'd better go check on Con," he reluctantly added.

She drew back, sniffling. "Okay."

Neil cocked his head, looking at her intently. Even crying she was beautiful. He lifted one finger to intercept a trailing tear. Then, hesitantly, he touched his lips to hers.

It took Robin a full second to respond, and he thought maybe he'd made a mistake. He started to turn away, apologize, but she then brought her hand up to his neck, her thumb brushing over the small bandage there, and kissed him back.

A long moment passed before he broke the contact. "I really should go find Conrad," he said, his forehead resting against hers, "but if it's okay, I would love to come back to this. Soon."

She laughed low in her throat. "Yeah, it's definitely okay." She laid a hand on his chest and leaned back to look him in the eye. "Go on," she said, tilting her head toward the door.

He kissed her lightly on the cheek before turning to leave.

———————

HE FOUND CONRAD IN the locker room, attacking a stain from the punch he'd splashed on the bottom of his shirt with a wadded up paper towel.

"I think it's dead now," Neil said.

Conrad's head snapped up, then he blew out a breath and continued to rub out the stain. "What do you want, Neil?"

"Me? Nothing. Except to make sure you're okay." Conrad only grunted in reply. "You wanna talk about it?"

"No," he said in a glum voice, not looking up.

Neil shrugged. "Suit yourself." He turned back toward the door.

"I guess the party's over," Conrad called after him before he took a third step.

Neil's mouth quirked in an almost smile before he stepped back into the locker room. "Yeah," he replied. "Everybody kinda just shuffled out, not really sure what to make of all of it."

"Well," Conrad said, throwing the paper towel into the nearest trash can, "I guess that's my fault, too."

"Too?"

He dropped to sit on the bench in front of his locker and ran his fingers through his hair. His expression when he looked back up cut Neil through to the heart. His eyes were red and he blinked to hold back tears. "It should've been me." His voice was barely controlled anguish.

"What should've been you?"

Conrad took a deep breath and let it out before answering. "We didn't know how much time we had. Frankie and Cal and I, we were trying to get everyone out. But then Cal saw something he thought was important and went back in... Frankie tried to stop him, but I - I just wanted out of there, man. And then the whole place blew and they -" He had his elbows on his thighs, his legs jouncing in agitation.

He shook his head as a few tears leaked down his cheeks. "I should have dragged them both out, but I ... I panicked, man. I ran." He sniffed. "Serves me right that I didn't get very far."

"You saw the fire bomb?"

"Frankie saw it, not long after he let us into the suite. It was in the fireplace. It looked like a pipe bomb connected to a can of gasoline or something - nothing huge and scary like you'd expect. All I could see was the detonator - it had a little red light blinking away at us. We couldn't tell if there was a timer or not, so we had no idea how much time we had or how much damage it would do..." His gaze was far away, his eyes reflecting the terror he must have felt in the moment. "Why didn't he just leave? Why didn't they both just get the hell out of there?" He rubbed a hand across his face. "Why didn't I stay?"

"Do you think that would have been better? Do you think if you had died - like you almost did anyway - or had been the one crippled or maimed, that it would have somehow been better?"

Conrad looked him in the eye, but his sight was still turned to that other time. "Maybe."

Neil closed the distance between them and backhanded Conrad across the face.

"What the hell, man?" Conrad demanded, putting a hand to his busted lip.

"Don't ever say that," Neil said harshly, almost shouting as raw emotion got past his tightly-controlled placid demeanor. "What happened in there is not on you. It is on Simon Turner and Tony Barrett. They are the ones who caused all this," he added in a hoarse, shaky voice, "so don't you dare put yourself alongside them. You're alive, Cal and Frankie are alive. We're *all* alive. God is not done with any of us yet, so you just cut this crap out. Do you hear me?"

Conrad, still cradling his bleeding lip, looked at him a stunned moment. "Yes," he said, his voice breaking. He swallowed and then repeated in a stronger voice, "Yes. I hear you."

Neil nodded and started to turn away, ashamed of the outburst, no matter how needed it might have been. But Conrad stood up and laid a hand on Neil's shoulder, staying him. "Neil," he said, "thank you."

Neil half turned and grabbed a paper towel out of the dispenser by the door and handed it to Conrad. "Here, clean yourself up. We've got work to do," he said with an apologetic smile. "Okay?"

Conrad took the towel with a quiet laugh. "Yeah, okay." He shoved Neil away jokingly and left the room, the towel pressed to his lip.

Neil stayed behind a moment longer, mastering his calm again. He shouldn't have hurt Conrad - that was way over the line. But he couldn't just let his best friend wallow in guilt, thinking what happened to Frankie and Parker was his fault. He had to snap him out of it. But still, lashing out like that...

Once he was calm once more, he went out to find Robin again. Maybe now, after that kiss, he could find the nerve to ask her out.

CHAPTER FORTY-EIGHT

———

FRANKIE WAS SLEEPING.

Noah almost left without disturbing him, but the sight of his friend lying in a hospital bed, with moistened dressings applied across his chest and upper arms, looking so... mortal, rooted him to the spot. Too many times he'd felt this same sense of helplessness and fear for people he cared about. And this past couple of weeks his emotions had been in constant overdrive so long he was starting to forget what it was like to feel relaxed and at peace.

Frankie began to stir restlessly, small sounds escaping from between his lips. Noah strode forward and touched his friend's clenched hand. Frankie's eyes snapped open and he gasped in panic, arms flailing.

"Frankie - Frankie, you're okay," Noah assured him. Frankie's eyes focused on Noah's face, still frightened and disoriented. "You're okay."

He gulped. "Noah?"

"Yeah, it's me. You all right now?"

He cleared his throat. "Yeah. It's... dreams." He looked around the room as if to reassure himself that he was, in fact, safe. "Uh, what are you doing here?"

"I came to see how you were doing, idiot."

He frowned. "Isn't there a rule about not insulting people in hospital beds?"

Noah laughed. "Probably. But it didn't make it into the law books, so..."

"Nice." He shifted uncomfortably, and examined the dressings on his arms. Then he looked up and prompted, "Speaking of legalities...?"

"Ah. The trial resumes next month. Branson has turned state's evidence, in exchange for reduced charges. Warner made a similar deal with Barrett - if he testifies against Turner, he'll get whatever time he needed on the stand to," he made air quotes, "tell the whole story. That was all he asked for, no plea bargain." He shook his head. "He's waiving his Fifth Amendment rights, just for the publicity, I think. He doesn't seem to care what it will mean for his own trial."

"The guy is nuts."

Noah shrugged. "He says he doesn't care what happens to him, as long as justice gets done. He wants history to record the tragedy at Brookview and Simon Turner's role in it."

Frankie scoffed. "Still trying to paint himself the avenging angel, huh? Never mind he killed a woman and put almost a dozen lives at risk."

"Don't worry, the light will be shined on the monster inside Barrett when it comes to his trial." Noah assessed his former partner's condition. He didn't seem to be in pain at the moment, and the panic of before had finally dissipated. "So, when you coming back to the station? I'm going to need some help moving into my big new office."

"What are you...? Are you back?"

"Sort of. Ziehring offered me the teaching gig. I assume I have you to thank for that."

Frankie grunted. "Took him long enough. I've only been suggesting it for months." He gave Noah a weak grin. "It'll be damn good to have you back in the house."

"It'll be damn good to be back. But like I said, I'm going to need help settling in, so you've got to get your butt out of this bed. Soon. You copy?"

Frankie smiled. "I copy."

CHAPTER FORTY-NINE

———

NIGHT HAD FALLEN OVER the city, as silently as ever. But tonight the city breathed a little easier, laughed more readily and slept more soundly than it had in weeks. The peace that had been shattered was mending once more, now those who had shattered it were locked away where they could no longer do so again.

The city slept.

In his cell, Simon Turner also slept. But, unlike the rest of the city, his sleep was not sound, not peaceful. In his cell, Simon Turner dreamt of fire.

And the screams of the dying filled his mind.

CHAPTER FIFTY

———

THE FEMALE NEWS ANCHOR tilted her stylishly coiffed head toward the camera as she switched over from one topic to the next.

"In other news, an update on real estate mogul Simon Turner's murder trial. It seems the tide has turned against the city's 'Golden Boy.' Today, after the final leg of testimony from former Riverdale police officer Daniel Branson - who was complicit in numerous acts of coercion and blackmail at Turner's behest but has now turned State's Evidence in exchange for a lighter sentence - and a strange, impassioned monologue from Joseph Anthony Barrett - an alleged arsonist who Turner first approached to set fire to his Brookview apartment building but declined for fear of endangering those who resided there - the jury and the entire city was able to see the ugly side of Simon Turner he didn't want us to know about."

The camera angle changed again, and she shifted her position to follow it, her over-powdered face appearing chalky in the unflattering studio lighting. "We go now to Brad outside the Calera County courthouse. Brad?"

The scene changed to show a lanky, older man in a tan suit who looked like he should be giving the sportscast instead of standing on the courthouse steps. "Thank you, Angela. After months of heel-dragging through motions and hearings, the final chapter of the Simon Turner murder trial has come to a close. The prosecution rested its case today and the jury heard closing arguments from both sides just after lunchtime this afternoon. All that's left is for the jury to deliberate and render their verdict. Turner's attorney issued a statement at the end of court today saying, 'I am confident justice will be done. My client maintains his innocence and we continue to hold out hope the jury will wisely see this is the truth.'

"However," he continued, the wind ruffling his light brown hair and chuffing into the microphone, "Prosecutor Gerald Warner had this to say:"

The lanky field reporter's feed was replaced by footage of Gerald Warner surrounded by the press outside the courthouse doors earlier in the day. He appeared calm and confident, dressed in a finely-tailored charcoal grey suit. "The defense has tried to paint a portrait of Simon Turner that the jury has now found out does not reflect his true nature. I have every confidence they have seen what kind of man he really is and will do the right thing: find him guilty of this horrible, horrendous crime."

———————

Convicted arsonist and murderer commits suicide

Riverdale - Simon Turner, age 43, was found dead in his cell in the Calera County Prison around 3:00 this morning of an apparent suicide. Turner was convicted this week in the arson that resulted in the deaths of almost two dozen residents of the Brookview Apartments building which Turner owned and managed. The apparent motive had been to collect on the building's insurance money, as the seemingly successful real estate mogul was severely in debt. Turner had also been indicted on additional charges of extortion, insurance fraud and criminal conspiracy and would face sentencing to the harshest of punishments, either life without parole or death by lethal injection. More details will follow as they are released.

In a related story, the trial of Joseph Anthony Barrett - charged in the attacks on firefighter Vincent Perry and Calera County Crime Lab criminalist Neil Coates, the death of Bell Memorial Hospital nurse Amy Simpson and the explosion that nearly claimed the lives of several members of the RPD and crime lab - is set to commence tomorrow. Barrett had testified against Simon Turner and was one of two key witnesses the prosecution credits with securing a guilty verdict. We'll have more on that story, too, as it develops.

Also by J.I. O'Neal:

<u>The Riverdale PD Series</u>

Impact: A Riverdale PD Series Prequel

Time of Death (Coming 2018)

Don't miss out!

Visit the website below and you can sign up to receive emails whenever J.I. O'Neal publishes a new book. There's no charge and no obligation.

https://books2read.com/r/B-A-MNEF-CBYP

BOOKS 2 READ

Connecting independent readers to independent writers.

Did you love *Indiscriminate: 5th Anniversary Revised Edition*? Then you should read *Time of Death* by J.I. O'Neal!

The clock was carved into her skin with care, the hand set at one o'clock, just like the others. The killer was telling them something, no doubt about that, but what exactly that something was, he couldn't begin to say.

In 2013, Detective Sergeant Noah Harkham suffered devastating and debilitating injuries that forced him into early retirement. Now, nearly a year later, he has found a new calling: teaching crime scene preservation techniques to the uniformed officers of his old precinct.

One case still haunts him, however. Eight years ago, Noah was a rookie detective working a gruesome case with his mentor and first partner, Rob Meares. Soon after Rob's unexpected death, the leads dried up and Noah was left with his first cold case. But now, after all these years, the killer has struck again, and Noah is called in to consult.

But when the evidence begins to point to Noah himself, he'll have to fight to clear his name and help his former partner and best friend, Detective Alan Franks, catch the real killer. Plagued with insomnia and bouts of uncharacteristic anger and erratic behavior, the cause of which even Noah doesn't understand, proving his innocence may end up being an insurmountable task- and his connection to the case is much more real than anyone could have imagined.